ALSO BY MICHAEL NEWTON

Gideon Thorn

Skinwalker

Leviathan Rising

Ghost Town

Mountain Devils

Soul Slayers

Hallowed Ground

Night Flyers

Empty Graves

RIP TIDE

RIP TIDE

A WEIRD WESTERN

GIDEON THORN
BOOK 9

MICHAEL NEWTON

Rip Tide
Paperback Edition
Copyright © 2026 (As Revised) by Michael Newton

Dark Wolf Books
An Imprint of Wolfpack Publishing
1707 E. Diana Street
Tampa, FL 33610

www.darkwolfbooks.com

All rights reserved. No part of this book may be reproduced in any form or by any electronic or mechanical means, including information storage and retrieval systems, without express written permission from the publisher, except for the use of brief quotations in reviews. Any use of this publication to train generative artificial intelligence (AI) technologies is expressly prohibited.

This book is a work of fiction. References to historical events, real people, or real places are used fictitiously. Any similarity to real persons, living or dead, is purely coincidental and not intended by the author.

All brand names and product names used in this book are trademarks, registered trademarks, or trade names of their respective holders. Wolfpack Publishing is not associated with any product or vendor in this book.

Paperback ISBN 979-8-89567-611-0
Ebook ISBN 9979-8-89567-610-3

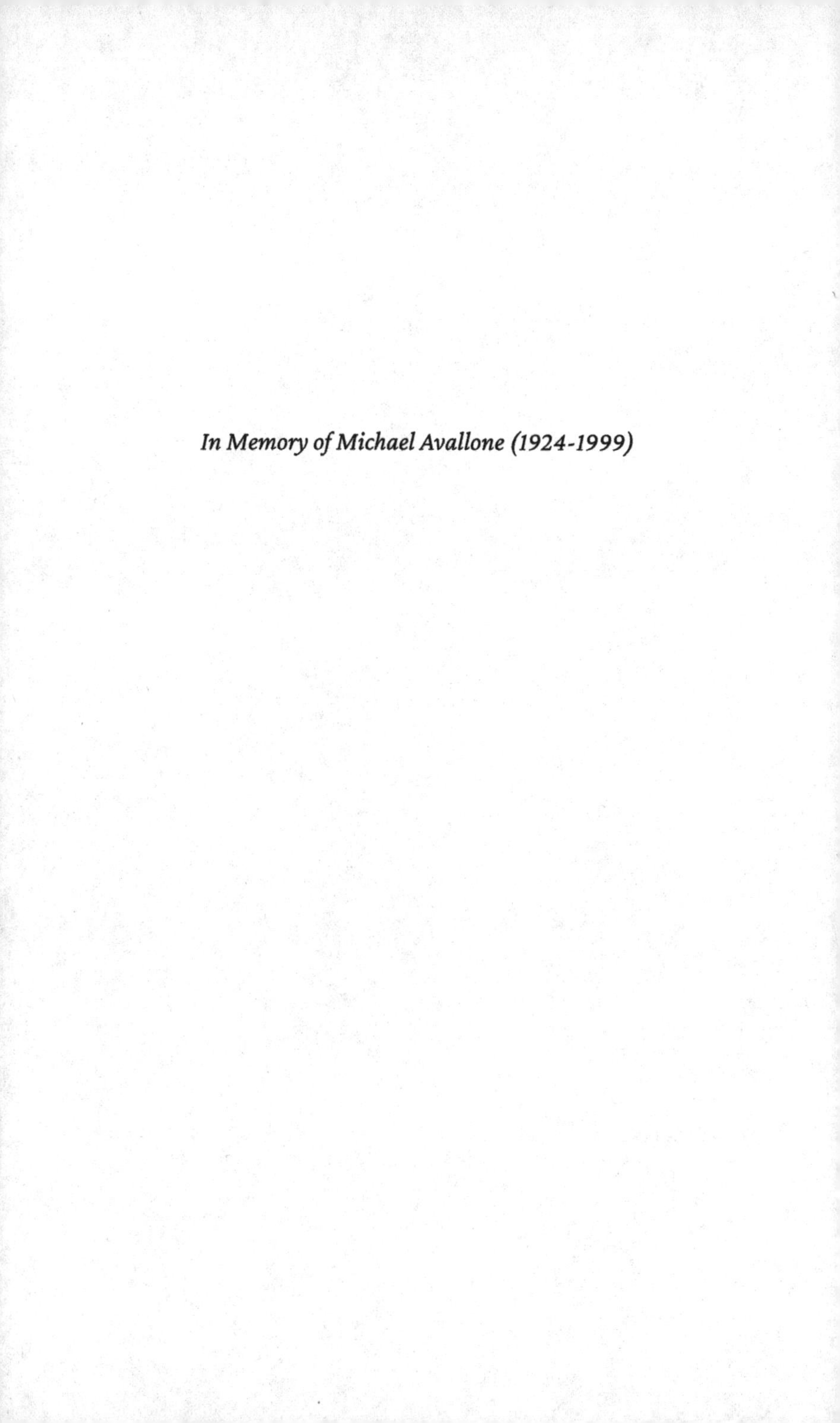

In Memory of Michael Avallone (1924-1999)

RIP TIDE

PROLOGUE

LOWER MISSISSIPPI RIVER: JUNE 11, 1877

First Mate Purnell Travis prowled the foredeck of the paddle steamer *Faust*, eyes scanning the dark river and the land away to either side.

To his left, eastward, Mississippi's shoreline was a dark expanse at half past midnight, most of Vicksburg's lights extinguished now, except around the district set aside for brothels and saloons. Off to the right, westward, the De Soto Peninsula thrust out from Louisiana's Madison Parish, forcing a bend in the river, narrowing its width to roughly a mile and one-half.

That was still plenty of room for the *Faust* to pass through, but her helmsman had to be careful. Night fishing, private and commercial, was a common pastime on the Mississippi, where unlicensed skippers often doused their running lights to keep from being spotted. Other passenger and cargo vessels also plied the river at all hours, some with better lamps aboard than others, and collisions were a common risk of travel on North America's "Father of Waters."

Most likely it was that concern that kept Travis awake tonight, beyond the normal hours of his watch, setting his nerves on edge.

And what else could it be?

For one thing, Travis didn't like the paddle steamer's name. He read few books, had never seen an opera, but Travis knew the old story of Faust all right, a man dissatisfied with his accomplishments in life who'd bargained with the Devil, selling off his soul for boundless knowledge and worldly pleasures. When the tab came due, of course, and Faust was carted off to an eternity in Hell, he could only blame himself.

Travis had known some men like that—and women, too. The truth be told, he still knew some such folk of both sexes and didn't mind their company, as long as he had booze on hand to mute the tiny voice of conscience nattering away inside his head.

The moral being that most things you might desire in life could be obtained, but only at a price.

What else was new?

Vicksburg, for instance, had grown filthy rich from slavery and cotton in its glory days, before the Civil War. Besieged by Yankee troops in 1863, the proud "Gibraltar of the Confederacy" held out for two months before surrendering, at a cost of some eight thousand persons killed, wounded or missing on both sides.

The war was bad enough, but only fourteen months ago, in April, the Mississippi shrugged and sliced across De Soto Peninsula, shearing off De Soto Point, destroying whatever General Ulysses Grant's troops had left of the Vicksburg, Shreveport and Texas Railroad terminal and ferry. That wiped out the region's east-west rail line and briefly left Vicksburg without a river—until, ironically, the U.S. Army Corps of Engineers, just three years old, arrived to set things right.

So, life went on for some, while others paid the price in lost lives, damaged health, and property destroyed.

Since Appomattox, steamboats known for hauling passengers along the Mississippi, some craft little more than brothels and casinos set afloat, had most made the shift to carrying bulk cargos south from St. Louis and Memphis to the Gulf of Mexico, then northward from New Orleans, hitting stops along the way at towns where merchants needed products for their stores, and growing postwar factories required an endless stream of raw materials.

Most times, the trips were uneventful. Sometimes there were arguments or brawls among crewmen, soon finding out that skippers took no guff from men on their payrolls and didn't mind tossing a troublemaker overboard to sink or swim to shore, sometimes a mile or more away. That didn't count as murder under river law, where any ship's master was Lord over his crew, and antebellum times has seen various tinhorn gamblers cast over the side for cheating, sometimes used for target practice from the decks above.

And when it came to missing bodies, Travis doubted that another river on the continent could match the Mississippi for its butcher's bill. Swimmers drowned with clockwork regularity, fishermen disappeared without a trace, and no one even tried to count the colored folks or their occasional white friends who wound up in the river wearing chains to weight them down.

Travis wondered, sometimes, whether the Mississippi washed away their sins or simply swept them on to Hell.

The first mate noted that his corncob pipe had died on him while he was ruminating at the *Faust*'s bow, and he was starting to refill it with Dutch shag tobacco—the *zware,* or "heavy" blend—when a tremor rocked the paddle wheeler and he nearly dropped his pipe over the rail.

Startled, Travis peered down into the dark river, saw nothing, then rushed to the starboard rail, fearing the pilot must have struck a hidden sandbar. If he had, and tried to forge ahead without reversing, it could crack the ship's hull, maybe even wreck the stern wheel in its wooden paddle box.

Nothing to starboard, so he hurried back the way he'd come, to check the ship's port side. When he was halfway there, another jolt—stronger this time—came close to putting Travis on his hands and knees. Shouting a curse up toward the wheelhouse, he recovered awkwardly and reached the left-hand railing, seeing water briefly foam along that side.

And nothing else.

Waiting, fearful of yet another shock that might rip through the steamer's keel, Travis clung to the rail and counted thirty seconds in his head, lips moving to keep track. When nothing happened in that time, he felt anger replacing fear and turned toward the *Faust*'s ladder—what landlubbers knew as stairs—to reach the upper deck and find out if the pilot had been dozing at the wheel, or if he was a clumsy simpleton.

Rage took him halfway up the ladder, then another, stronger jolt rattled the steamer, caused a tilt to port that made him curse again, then hurry on to reach the upper deck. From there, he had a better view to starboard and imagined that he glimpsed the sandbar they were scraping, longer than the *Faust* itself, although the new moon cast no light to help him see.

When Travis reached the bridge, be pushed his way inside and found the pilot—Arnett Dillon, ten years younger than himself, still wet behind the ears—gaping at him and asking, "What in hell was that?"

"You didn't see it?"

"Can't see shit, a night like this," the wheelman answered back. "It just—"

Before Dillon could finish saying whatever he meant to vocalize, the steamer took its strongest hit so far and started rising on its starboard side, as if preparing to capsize.

Swearing a blue streak, Travis fled the wheelhouse, stumble-slid down the port ladder on his backside, landing in a heap on the main deck. He scrabbled to the rail on all fours, grabbed it, drew himself into a standing posture, and stared down into the Mississippi.

Just in time to see it staring back at him.

The shock of that, the sheer insanity of it, made Travis yelp a strangled cry of panic and recoil, loping across the deck to starboard, trying to escape from whatever it was that he'd just seen.

Cold sober as he was, the first mate wished that he was drunk. At least that might explain the vision that he guessed would haunt him to the End of Days.

Where was he going? Travis didn't know and hardly cared, as long as he was moving, putting space between himself and what he prayed had been only a waking nightmare.

And with that thought barely formed, the paddle steamer took another hit that pushed it halfway over toward the starboard side. Travis could barely stay upright, lurching across the deck until the railing struck him in the gut and he flipped over it, wailing as he plunged into dark, swift water, with the *Faust* rolling on top of him.

ONE

NATCHEZ, MISSISSIPPI: JUNE 11, 1877

The ferry from Vidalia, Louisiana, bumped against its designated pier extending from the Natchez waterfront. A burly, bearded man leapt from its deck, trailing a hawser line that he made fast around a rusty stanchion at dockside. Another line was cast off from the ferry's stern and knotted to a second upright metal post.

It took another moment for a second member of the ferry's crew to lower and secure its wooden loading ramp and signal it was safe for passengers to go ashore. Gideon Thorn hung back, letting the customers who'd brought no animals aboard to go ahead of him, then followed with his jet-black stallion, Shadow, and his molly pack mule, Bell.

It was good to be on solid ground again, albeit in a city Thorn had never visited before. His animals had both disliked the ferry ride across from Concordia Parish, but they calmed immediately, Thorn eavesdropping on their thoughts as he had learned to do in childhood, following his family's demise, while he was living at a Kansas orphanage.

Now, rounding off this twenty-fifth year on the planet, Thorn was used to that—though still confused on why some species were closed off to him entirely—and he had grown used to many other things as well, some which he wished he'd never seen.

Mounting Shadow, trailing Bell's lead line, Thorn passed along the waterfront, seeking his prearranged hotel, the Haverstock Hilltop on Silver Street, featuring a river view and stable on the premises. The streets were crowded, forcing Thorn to navigate around buckboards and other horsemen, dead-axle dray wagons, and pedestrians who milled about at random, some stopping to stare as Thorn passed by.

He was a sight to see, at six foot four and sitting ramrod-straight in Shadow's saddle. Thorn was clad in black from flat-brimmed had to knee-high boots, the sole exception a white dress shirt worn beneath his coat and vest. Around his sender waist, he wore a pistol belt supporting twin Colt Single Action Army "Peacemakers," chambered for the same .44-40 rounds used by the Winchester Model 1873 rifle in his saddle boot.

His other long gun, riding Bell, wrapped up in buckskin for concealment and protection from the elements, was an 1872 Sharps rifle in .50-90 caliber, accurate to one thousand yards with the two-foot telescopic sight mounted atop its thirty-two-inch barrel.

And if all else failed, Thorn also packed two knives. A Bowie with a twelve-inch blade was sheathed behind his back, a shorter dagger, double-edged, protruding from its scabbard in his right-hand boot.

A casual observer might have said he was prepared for

anything, but Thorn knew that was only an illusion. Most days slapped him with some new surprise as Gideon traveled the country, looking for solutions to unsolved—and often deadly—mysteries.

That quest began when he was barely two years old, the night an unknown creature massacred his parents and his elder brother, sparing Thorn's life but leaving him with psychic and physical scars. Some of the cases he'd investigated led to apprehension of sadistic human perpetrators; others had propelled him to the very edge of reason and beyond.

And while he had discovered partial answers to the many questions haunting him, he was confronted by a universe of riddles, each in turn to be confronted as they came, at risk to life and limb.

Eleven months ago, he'd put paid to the creature that had slain his family—or maybe one of its descendants—with the aid of two close friends. Obi Magoro hailed from Africa, brought back by Thorn's grandfather as a servant, now custodian of Gideon's inherited estate, sole year-round occupant of the family's mansion on Beacon Hill, in Boston. Obi was a stranger to him when Thorn's Aunt Drusilla sent to retrieve her only living relative and heir from the "children's home" where Gideon had languished since his family's slaughter. Fed up with bullies, Thorn had learned a range of martial arts from Obi that included Dambe bare-knuckle boxing, Engolo ritual combat, and Nguni stick-fighting.

His other helper during last year's showdown with the past was Dinah Pilcher, a lady journalist and editor of her own newspaper in San Diego, California, when she'd crossed Gideon's path during a spate of grisly human sacrifices meant to end the world as white men knew it. They'd been something more than friends while traveling together after that, Dinah collecting information for a book that would—she hoped—reveal the truth of Thorn's strange odyssey, unique in modern times. She's lent a hand in Colorado Territory, taking down the monster of his dreams, then they had separated while she chased more outré stories and had nearly lost her life—if not her soul—just three months earlier in rural Arkansas.

That close encounter with Voodoo and the alleged "undead" had nearly broken Dinah, but she had been fighting back since then, sequestered with Obi Magoro in the house on Beacon Hill, treated by top-rated physicians and alienist who refused to write her off as "crazy" or "hysterical." According to his latest telegrams from Obi and a letter penned by Dinah, she'd come through the worst of it, reclaimed most of her mind and life, considering whether the time had come for her to strike off on her own once more.

The treatments she'd required had been expensive, but money was one thing Thorn didn't have to fret about. His grandfather had been a wealthy and unmarried man, left all his worldly goods to Aunt Drusilla, and she'd passed them down in turn to Gideon. Before her death, she'd seen him through Boston's Weatherford Academy and Harvard University, graduating with a bachelor's degree at twenty-one. From there, he'd planned on Harvard Law, but changed his mind when Aunt Drusilla died, seeing an opportunity to find out what had killed his family and, in the process, solve more puzzles of a life defying simple logic.

Aunt Drusilla Thorn had been an ardent spiritualist, in addition to a canny businesswoman who'd increased her father's fortune many times over. Her fascination with the

"Other Side" had stuck with Gideon, who shied away from any one dogmatic faith but wore the emblems of five —a small cross, Star of David, crescent moon of Islam, pentagram of Wicca, and a feather for First Nations' animism—on a silver chain around his neck, under his shirt.

It was past noon, according to his pocket watch, when Gideon reined in before the Haverstock Hilltop hotel. Dismounting, he looped Shadow's reins and Bell's lead line over the hotel's hitching rail, passed silent explanations to the stoic animals, and made his way inside.

A short clerk with red hair and a distinctive overbite perked up at Thorn's appearance in the lobby, barely glancing at the new arrival's weapons, putting on a smile he'd probably rehearsed in front of mirrors at his home.

"Good afternoon, sir! Welcome to the Haverstock Hilltop. How may I serve you?"

"I should have a reservation," Gideon replied, "confirmed by wire two days ago."

The clerk glanced at a bulky register in front of him and ran his index finger down the page, stopping near the bottom. "Mr. Thorn?"

"That's me."

"How long will you be staying with us, sir?"

"I'm not sure yet," Thorn said. "Two or three days, at least. I may need to extend that."

Predictions weren't a skill that he'd inherited. Arriving in a new town might meet rapid disappointment, finding out that stories of an incident reported in the press had either been exaggerated or made up from thin air to fill "silly season" column inches. On the other hand, he might be stepping into an abyss from which there would be no escape.

A crapshoot, and it only took one roll of snake-eyes to spell doom.

"Excellent, sir," the manager replied. "I'm Andre, hours six a.m. to six p.m., six days a week. Some call me Mr. Six-Six-Six."

Thorn nearly frowned at that but let it go, the manager's quick laugh assuring Gideon that it was just a joke. He smiled along and signed the register upon request, received a key with "No. 5" engraved on its brass fob, and said, "If someone's covering your stable, I have two animals tied outside."

"Yes, sir. Of course. It's down the alley to your left as you step out, and then around in back. Our hostler, Kelsey Underhill, will get them situated for you."

Thorn followed directions, led his animal companions through a gate that closed off access to the yard and barn behind for idle passersby. He soothed them with bland thoughts, moving along an alley paved with bricks set into soil, and found a barn behind the Haverstock Hilltop with its door open, six or the eight stalls inside awaiting customers.

Kelsey the hostler had a round head, planted on thick shoulders, with a round torso below, reminding Thorn of a snowman who'd come to life—except that he was black, with graying hair and sideburns. He refrained from offering a hand to Thorn, a symptom of the racial mores Gideon had dealt with anytime he crossed the Mason-Dixon Line. Instead of forcing it, Thorn pitched in, helping him unsaddle Shadow and remove the packs Bell had been carrying.

That done, Thorn saw them into stalls with feed and water readily available, then made the first of two trips back inside the Haverstock, bearing his rifles and his saddle bags, leaving some of the other bundled gear for last.

When he passed through the lobby with his rifles, manager Andre ventured, "Come to Natchez for the hunting, sir? We have some prime big game about."

"I hope you're right," Thorn said, already on the stairs, and let it go at that.

His room was adequate. The water closet came as a surprise to Thorn, who had been wondering about the hotel's lack of privy in its fenced-off yard. Beyond that, it came furnished with a four-poster bed, an armoire, chest of drawers, a vanity table and mirror, plus a single straight-backed wooden chair. Its single window offered him the promised river view, but barely. Most of what he saw from there was waterfront, with steamers and their smokestacks blocking visual examination of the Mississippi.

Fair enough. He'd need a closer look regardless, in his own good time.

Thorn stowed his rifles in the armoire, then distributed the contents of his saddle bags, spare shirts and such filling a couple of the dresser's drawers. An accordion file folder gave up correspondence and his latest crop of clippings from newspapers which had put him on the scent of his intending job.

He'd found the first piece in the *Arkansas Gazette* and it had piqued his interest, reporting on a "serpent" that had swamped a sailboat on the Mississippi, either drowning or devouring its three-man crew. In either case, the victims were still missing—not unusual for swimmers in the in the mighty Mississippi—and descriptions of the "monster" had been gleaned from an intoxicated man on shore, near dusk. Neither the newspaper nor lawmen from the nearest river town—Helena, Arkansas—appeared to give the story any credence.

Next came an item from the *Memphis Commercial Appeal,* sarcastically alluding to reports of "boss snake" seen swimming downstream past Friar's Point, Mississippi, frightening four picnickers into a state of near hysteria. More sightings had been logged from Greenville, Arkansas City, and Eudora. None claimed any loss of human life, although a fisherman out of Lake Providence, Louisiana, swore he'd seen the creature swallowing an alligator close to shore. He'd signed an affidavit swearing to the truth of that, but no one from the East Carroll Parish sheriff's office cared enough to check it out.

And then, most recently, had come a story from the *Vicksburg Daily Herald*, saying that the paddle steamer *Faust* had run afoul of something unidentified, while bearing cargo back from Memphis to Natchez. Of seven men aboard, the captain and five others were listed as missing and presumed lost. One—the first mate, named in print as Purnell Travis—claimed a huge beast had attacked the *Faust* and wrecked it. He'd survived coincidentally, by falling overboard and swimming for his life.

Night fishermen had seen the *Faust* capsize and float away downstream, its keel topmost until it rammed the shore a few miles north of Natchez. One witness surmised that it had struck a sandbar, while another claimed the *Faust* had run down an unlighted barge. Warren County's sheriff said both were mistaken; there was no sandbar, no barge reported missing, and no wreckage from a second vessel.

Nothing but a mystery that challenged Thorn and put him on the trail to Natchez, thankful to be leaving Arkansas.

He had come close to dying in the Razorback State, and Dinah Pilcher had come closer still. In truth, Thorn couldn't swear that part of her had not crossed over to the afterlife his Aunt Drusilla had pursued until the day she died.

If there was any mystery to solve beyond the grave, Gideon reckoned that Drusilla knew its answers now. If there was not...well, he would have to wait and find out for himself one day.

Now Dinah was recuperating from her Arkansas ordeal, making advances daily in Obi Magoro's view, and while Thorn missed her, he was glad to know that she was safe and sound in Boston while he chased leads to another riddle that might take him nowhere.

And if witnesses were right about some massive unknown creature lurking in the Mississippi, what did he propose to do about it?

Thorn had no idea, but realized that he was hungry now, with no food having passed his lips since breakfast near the crack of dawn. That had been eggs and grits in Jenna, seat of La Salle Parish, and while he had savored it, his stomach was complaining now, demanding sustenance.

Scanning the room before he left, Thorn locked the door behind him and descended to the hotel lobby facing Silver Street.

He walked to Pepper Jack's Steak House and found it moderately busy with lunch trade. Most of the diners eyeballed Thorn while he stood waiting for the blonde waitress to notice him and bustle over, smiling more from force of habit than enjoyment of her work.

Gideon knew exactly how he looked to those Natchezians, a well-armed stranger dressed as for a funeral, meeting their eyes until the locals had enough of it and turned away. Once he was seated at a window table meant for two, Thorn doffed his hat and almost smiled at the reactions from his fellow diners.

Thorn's jet-black hair was parted down the middle, with a blaze of white tracing the scar a monster had inflicted on him at the age of two, before it massacred his family. Gideon still had no idea why it allowed him to escape that night. It could have run him down with ease, devoured him in half a dozen bites, but Fate or pure dumb luck had spared his life and ultimately set him on his present path.

The waitress handed him a menu, left him to peruse it, and came back with coffee in a large ceramic mug. Thorn opted for a T-bone steak, a baked potato, with a salad on the side and sipped the strong black coffee while she went to place his order with the cook. Rather than match stares with the other customers again, he watched traffic on Silver Street and thought about the stories that had brought him there, how he should try to prove them true or false.

Thorn already knew what his next stop would be after lunch. He had an address for the daily *Natchez Independent* and was hoping that its editor might have fresh information on the incidents reported during recent weeks. Whether said editor would see Thorn or agree to help him was another question that could only be resolved in person.

And if that approach failed him...what, then?

Thorn had no other angles of attack in mind so far, but guessed that speaking to the Adams County sheriff of the town's chief of police might be in order, even if that proved to be another waste of time.

Thorn missed his home in Boston, though he'd rarely been there since his epic tour of the West and South began.

More than the mansion and its trappings, he missed spending time with Obi Magoro and with Dinah Pilcher, now that she seemed to be on the mend.

At least, he hoped that was the truth, but Gideon had spent his life grappling with trauma suffered as a child. How much more difficult would Dinah's road back be for her, when she'd been stripped of all free will as an adult, when she was long accustomed to deciding matters for herself, succeeding in a world that looked to men first for accepted leadership?

Thorn didn't have a clue how it must feel to have one's mind enslaved, but he'd tried to imagine it, albeit unsuccessfully. Today, he wasn't sure if being in proximity to Dinah would assist in her recovery or only make things worse. Maybe her doctor could advise him, through Obi, and Thorn could lay his plans from there.

Whatever, Boston would just have to wait. The manse on Beacon Hill was fifteen hundred miles northeast of Natchez, and Thorn couldn't undertake that journey until he had decided for himself whether the latest Mississippi River tales were true or false.

If it was all a sham, compounded by coincidence, so be it. Gideon had wasted time before, and doubtless would again. But if the claims proved out, then action was required.

And he had no idea of how he might proceed.

His meal arrived, the steak smothered in grilled onions and mushrooms—a bonus—while the baked potato's skin was seasoned with a coat of garlic salt. The salad, dressed with vinegar and oil, was large enough to be a meal all by itself, but Thorn was ravenous and put it all away over the next half hour, with a slice of pecan pie to round things off.

When he was halfway through the meal, who should

appear but Pepper Jack himself, a beefy man sporting a handlebar mustache and sideburns, compensating for a hairline that was in retreat. He introduced himself as Jacque Beauchamp, his French accent suggesting he'd been raised somewhere in Cajun country.

"How you find your meal today?" he asked.

"It's perfect," Thorn assured him.

"Dat's what I was tryin' for. You're new around dese parts, I think—or leastways, new to Pepper Jack's."

"You're right on both counts," Thorn admitted. "Passing through."

"I hope you find the time to stop with us again, Mister—?"

Thorn introduced himself and the shook hands, Beauchamp prepared to move on, circulating through the dining room, but Thorn delayed him for a moment with a question.

"Is it possible that you could help me out?"

"Wit what?" the chef inquired.

"I'm looking into some reports of incidents along the river," Gideon replied.

"Ah, *oui*. You mean de great *monster de mers,* eh?"

Thorn spoke enough French to get along in high society back east and recognized the phrase for "sea monster." It didn't seem to fit a river-dwelling creature, but he saw no point in arguing semantics with the chef.

Nodding, he asked, "What do you think about the stories?"

"Well, sir, I don't wanna say they true o' false, but people have been seein' strange things on the Mississippi since she was discovered by de Soto and de red men got they stories goin' even farther back. Myself, I ain't seen nothin' but some gators and a mighty big stingray one time, about a bull's size if you can believe it. Didn't try to spear it, though, so doubt me if you wanna."

Thorn knew giant stingrays, growing more than six feet long and weighing up to thirteen hundred pounds, were sometimes found in Asia, while unverified reports of others had been logged from Africa and South America. Some were restricted to freshwater; others seemed to be at ease in lakes and rivers or at sea.

"So, nothing large enough to sink a paddle steamer, then?" he asked Beaumont.

"You talk about de *Faust* now, eh? My thinkin' is—don't quote me, now—de pilot likely had a snoot full and jest run aground."

"And the survivor? What about his story?"

" 'Story's' what I call it, sure. Maybe de whole crew spend de night drinkin', or that one who fall overboard jest seen a log, a gator, who knows what-all?"

Nodding, Thorn thanked Beauchamp for his time and turned back to his meal.

He put no special stock in Pepper Jack's opinion, although it was logical enough. And if a giant beast habitually plied the Mississippi, Gideon supposed it stood to reason that the chef would pick up stories of it from his customers.

And yet...

Finished at last, he paid the waitress, got a true smile for his extra dollar tip, and left the restaurant.

Next stop: to see a man who lived for gathering and spreading news.

TWO

The *Natchez Independent* was a weekly newspaper, published on Fridays, that reminded Thorn a bit of Dinah Pilcher's *Sagrado Sentinel*, the paper she'd run by herself in California's San Diego County when their paths first crossed.

Granted, the *Independent*'s office was a little larger than the *Sentinel*'s had been, its door half glass, the wooden portion painted red to make it stand out from the other offices and shops along North Canal Street. And its editor—one Jubal Kenfield—was a man, as Gideon had learned from his research while on the road from Arkansas to Mississippi. As to what kind of man he was, and how he dealt with strangers operating own patch, was a question yet to be resolved.

Thorn entered through the red door, ready for the jangling of a small bell mounted overhead to warn the paper's backroom workers of a new arrival. He decided it was backroom *worker*, singular, when a man's voice called out, "Be with you in a second!"

More like two minutes has passed when a short, stocky

man emerged from the backroom, wiping his hands on an old ink-stained rag. He wore a green eyeshade and garters on the sleeves of his white shirt, resembling a casino dealer as much as a printer. His eyes were sharp behind a pair of wire-rimmed spectacles, the left side of his jaw and throat marked by a port-wine birthmark.

"Can I help you?" he inquired, after a twitchy glance at Thorn's two holstered Colts.

"Could be," Thorn said. "I hope to have a word with Jubal Kenfield."

"In the flesh," the birthmarked man replied. He offered Thorn a hand that Gideon deemed clean enough to shake, while he completed their brief introduction.

"Thorn?" the newsman echoed, as if talking to himself. "Gideon Thorn? Why does that sound familiar? Wait, don't tell me, now. You wouldn't be that fella who rides all around the country solving mysteries and such?"

"Guilty as charged," said Thorn. "But I'm surprised you've heard of me."

"I've *read* about you, sir, and with great interest I must say, following that syndicated series from the lady journalist. Her name was...let me think, now..."

"Dinah Pilcher," Thorn supplied, hoping to move their talk along.

"Of course! She had a nifty turn of phrase," Kenfield replied. "Our Mississippi dailies haven't carried any of her stories for a while, but I keep watching for then."

"She's been indisposed," Thorn said, hoping to let it go at that. "As to the reason why I'm interrupting you..."

"No interruption, sir. I've got the best part of two days to get the *Independent* out, all local trivia, and I can guess what's brought you to the Trace City."

"That's one I haven't heard before," said Gideon.

"Comes from the Natchez Trace, a forest trail that used to link us up with Nashville. Tennessee, that is, not Mississippi's Nashville in Lowndes County, pretty much a ghost town now."

"All right."

"And if I were a betting man, which I *am not*, I'd wager you were here about the river's so-called sea serpent."

"You'd be a winner," Thorn said.

"I wrote an editorial about it that you may have seen, after the *Faust* fetched up on shore."

"I haven't read it," Thorn admitted, "but I'm hoping to, along with any other articles you've run about the rumored incidents."

Kenfield's eyes widened for a second, then he said, "Agreed, sir. But there'd have to charge you for it."

Thorn was reaching for his billfold, nodding, as he said, "That's not a problem. Shall we say a year's subscription in advance?"

Kenfield raised a hand to stop him, saying, "You mistake my meaning, sir. The price would be an interview, exclusive, for my paper."

"Happy to oblige," said Gideon. "Although, the way I normally proceed, I wouldn't want it coming out this Friday, while I'm still investigating."

"Done and done!" said Kenfield, thrusting out his hand to shake a second time. With that accomplished, he opened a gate in the front counter of his office, saying, "If you'd kindly follow me into the morgue..."

If they'd been standing anywhere except the office of a newspaper, Thorn might have balked at that, but in their present situation he knew "morgue" to mean the paper's archives of back issues and assorted other reference materials.

He followed Kenfield to the backroom, past an offset lithographic printing press invented by an Englishman named Robert Barclay two years earlier. Beyond that, in a smaller, somewhat musty storage room, Kenfield had shelved bound volumes of the *Independent* with dates printed on the spine of each volume, four tomes per year, divided quarterly, that dated back to summer 1866.

"Don't worry," Kenfield said, as Gideon was ticking off the forty-odd volumes, hoping that he wouldn't have to page through all of them. "I've only logged reports about the creature going back to March, plus certain notes gleaned from the dailies out of Little Rock, Memphis, Jackson and Vicksburg."

"That should be a help," Thorn granted.

"And I'll gladly answer any questions you might have, of course."

"That's very generous."

"In rapt anticipation of your interview," Kenfield reminded him.

"I won't forget," Thorn said.

"I wouldn't let you," said the newsman, with another glance at Thorn's pistols. "Respectfully, of course. I take for granted that it's more exciting than the ladies' social planned for Saturday at Free Will Baptist Church."

Only two volumes of the *Independent* covered stories on reported sightings of the river monster. Kenfield had a list of publication dates to speed things up, and he also produced a file of clippings from the larger papers he'd referred to, plus three foolscap pages filled with notes in tidy longhand penmanship, then left his guest to read it all.

The story that unfolded had its roots in March, as

Kenfield had described, around the same time Thorn had been fighting to rescue Dinah Pilcher from a Voodoo priest in Arkansas. He'd missed the early stories, and was grateful to catch up on them, plus new details of the *Faust* disaster nine days previous.

Kenfield's notes and clippings from out-of-state papers were even more interesting. "Monster" sightings also issued from the White River, a major tributary of the Mississippi spanning 720 miles of Missouri and Arkansas, including swampy land along its course that rivaled the Louisiana bayous for gloomy expansiveness. Descriptions varied from those witnesses, and likewise from the broad Ohio River, winding some 980 miles from southwest Pennsylvania down to southern Illinois, where it connected to the Mississippi.

Each river in turn claimed humans and livestock with clockwork regularity, some of the victims found, an equal number lost without a trace. In theory, Thorn reckoned it was possible for some aquatic beast to travel inland from the Gulf of Mexico and wind its way along a river network that also included Mississippi's Big Black River, the Arkansas River, the Show-Me State's Missouri and Meramec Rivers, the Kaskaskia in Illinois, the Minnesota and Wisconsin Rivers, with a host of other tributaries across the Midwest.

All that territory beckoned an unknown tourist, assuming the creature existed and that it could survive in freshwater after being spawned at sea.

Certain stingrays aside, Thorn also knew of other species that could live either in fresh or saltwater. Among them were the American eel, barramundi or Asian sea bass, bull sharks, herrings, sockeye salmons, white perch and desert pupfish, among others. There was even a saltwater crocodile, largest of the alligator's living relatives, exceeding twenty feet in length, weighing a ton or more. Naturally ranging from Southeast Asia to Australia and the Philippines, the huge crocs fed on anything that came their way and could be swallowed whole or dragged under and drowned, including human beings.

While none of those reptiles had reached the Western Hemisphere as far as Thorn knew, they had a relative of nearly equal size in the American crocodile, found along Dixie's Gulf Coast and points south, including both coasts of Mexico, throughout the Caribbean, to Venezuela and Peru. Again, as with their Far East cousins, crocodiles in the Americas were sometimes maneaters, but Thorn had trouble picturing one large enough to wreck a steamer, even if its body got snagged by a paddle wheel.

So, what was left? A real-life giant snake, perhaps?

Thorn's study of zoology at Harvard had informed him that the not-so-New World's largest serpent was *Eunectes murinus*, the green anaconda of South America, found east of the Andes from Colombia and Venezuela, through Guiana, Ecuador, Peru, Bolivia and Brazil, plus the Caribbean islands of Trinidad and Tobago. Five subspecies were smaller, but *E. murinus* was Earth's heaviest known snake and the second longest, after Asia's reticulated python. Herpetologists assumed that it sometimes exceeded thirty feet in length, although the largest specimen on record measured twenty-nine and weighed 550 pounds.

Still, claims of truly giant anacondas, some triple the record length or more, had been recorded out of South America from early days of Portuguese and Spanish exploration to more recent tales of white explorers in the region, none providing skins or bones to verify their claims.

Thorn didn't rule a huge snake our, by any means—particularly after his encounter with a flying dragon in the wilds of southwest Texas—but he wasn't taking anything on faith alone, either. The Texas creature he'd surmised to be a prehistoric throwback or survivor, and the fossil record known by now included several aquatic reptiles of tremendous size and rabid appetite. Misguided authors often called those swimming creatures dinosaurs, a term that properly applied only to land-dwelling reptiles active between the Triassic and Cretaceous periods, 243 to 201 million years ago.

While *dinosaur* translated from Greek as "terrible lizard," size was in fact irrelevant. Some species known from fossilized remains had been no larger than a modern barnyard chicken, while the largest had exceeded eighty feet—so large, in fact, that specimens required a secondary "brain" inside their pelvises, to keep their hindquarters from dragging helplessly along.

As swimming prehistoric reptiles were not truly dinosaurs, so neither were their relatives with leather wings, who'd ruled the skies in ancient times, the pterosaurs, whose various wingspans had ranged from ten inches to thirty-odd feet. As with the tales of giant anacondas, stories out of Africa and elsewhere claimed that giant flying reptiles still survived today, dwelling in mountain caves and jungle hideaways where natives feared to go and white explorers rarely trespassed or returned alive.

Thorn didn't need to watch for flying beasts this time around, or giants plodding overland. Whatever he was seeking—if it wasn't just a pipedream—lived in water and pursued its prey there.

And he couldn't shake the question. *What in hell, if anything, would it turn out to be?*

• • •

Police Chief Halbert Hightower stared at the *Natchez Independent*'s office, wishing he could eavesdrop on the conversation underway behind its closed red door.

Hightower might have looked suspicious, lurking in the alleyway between a lawyer's office and a ladies' haberdashery on North Canal Street, opposite the newspaper, but he was a familiar sight around Natchez, forever on the move and turning up in uniform regardless of the hour, even on his putative days off.

Natchez was rife with vice of every kind, from its saloons and gambling halls to brothels, and while savvy operators paid their sin tax to the city on a monthly basis, interloping rogues were numerous and had to be curtailed out of respect for those who bought protection on a steady basis.

Beyond that, the waterfront witnessed no end of brawls and stabbings, thefts of cargo, even the occasional attempt to steal a riverboat. In "colored town," across the railroad tracks from white and more-or-less respectable Natchez, Hightower's officers ignored most crimes except for homicide, preserving energy to pounce like hungry panthers if a black man dared assault, insult, or otherwise offend his pale-skinned masters. Petty theft was rampant on commercial streets, and even stately homes that had survived the war fell prey to burglars now and then. The city's last armed robbery had taken place two months ago and ended in a blaze of gunfire with the would-be bandits shot to hell.

There was, of course, another kind of crime in Natchez, as throughout the state of Mississippi and the world at large. Men beat their wives and children, but police were only called if death resulted or the sluggers were confined to lower strata of society with no great reputations to protect. Hightower knew or strongly suspected families engaged in incest, but the victims seldom dared complain, and children spawned by misfit pairings usually "went away" somehow.

The brooding fear of post-war Mississippi was the image of a feral black man lusting for white women. Accusations of an interracial rape—not counting colored women ravaged by white men, of course—could spark a riot within hours, and few black suspects lived long enough to be convicted by an all-white jury and delivered to a white hangman. Before secession, 40 percent of Adams County's population had been slaves. Now freed, at least in theory, they were viewed by most whites as an ever-present threat, with lynch mobs standing ready to ensure that "order" was preserved.

That same job, with a twist, had brought Chief Hightower to spy on Jubal Kenfield's visitor this afternoon. The man in black—signed in as Gideon Thorn at the Haverstock Hilltop—had raised eyebrows from the moment that he'd disembarked that morning on the ferry's pier. He dressed in black like an outlaw and carried guns to spare, no crime in Natchez yet, and rumors had been circulating for the past few hours as to what his business might be and how long he planned to stay.

Most of the muttered speculation was pure bullshit, obviously, but Chief Hightower was paid to keep a lid on any trouble that disturbed his city's Upper Crust, and while he made more money monthly from the red light district's payoffs than his salary, he meant to keep his job no matter what it took.

When Thorn was finished at the *Independent,* Hightower would follow him wherever he went next, see who else he was talking to if anyone, then double back to find out what he wanted out of Jubal Kenfield. That was marginally risky, since the U.S. Constitution's first amendment promised freedom of the press, speech, and association, but so what?

In case Kenfield forgot, he was a citizen of Mississippi, most of whose white residents regarded as distinct and separate from the United States. Those merchants, voters and the like agreed that if the Yankee Constitution meant exactly what it said, ex-slaves would have the vote by now across the South, instead of being silenced at the polls, and there would be no binding labor contracts that effectively confined them to the cottonfields.

That was a lesson worth remembering, and Hightower would put it bluntly to the *Independent's* publisher if a reminder was required.

"You've given me a lot to think about," Thorn told Kenfield.

"Glad I could help a little, if at all," the publisher replied. "About our quid pro quo..."

"I'm not forgetting," Gideon assured him. "First, though, is it true that the only survivor from the *Faust* lives here in Nashville."

"Purnell Travis," Kenfield said. "Not right in town, but on the northeast outskirts. I can give you his address, but there's no guarantee he'll talk to you."

"Taking it hard, is he?" Thorn asked.

"I guess he lost some friends, all right, but it's the way townies have treated him that's mostly put him off."

"They doubt his story?"

"That's putting it mildly," Kenfield said, frowning. "Between kids jeering at him on the street, their parents calling him a drunkard, lunatic and liar, I'm surprised he hasn't packed up and moved on. My guess would be it's down to Armond Joslin, Travis staying on in Natchez."

"Who's this Joslin?" Gideon inquired.

"He owns the Natchez & New Orleans Line—shipping, that is—with two, three dozen steamers working from the Gulf on up to Memphis and beyond. One less, now that he's lost the *Faust*."

"And those crewmen."

"He's covering the funerals for families that won't reject an act of charity, but two or three have turned him down on principle, for what it's worth."

"Do you suppose he'd speak to me?"

The newsman rolled his shoulders in a lazy shrug. "He let me interview him on the accident, gave me some details on the cargo lost and names of missing crewmen, but he's been an advertiser and subscriber to the *Independent* since I set up shop. Whether he'll say much to a stranger, I don't know."

Still worth a try, Gideon thought, but kept that to himself. He wouldn't pressure Kenfield for an introduction that might backfire and reduce the paper's normal revenue.

"I'll start with Travis," he replied, "and go from there. You said the *Faust* landed a few miles north of Natchez?"

"Two, three miles approximately," Kenfield estimated. "Still sitting there for now. Ride north along the riverbank and you can't miss it, with the way it's wedged in from the current, upside down. I'm guessing that its stacks are jammed into the mud along there. It'll likely take a crew with axes to dismantle it and haul away whatever's left."

"I'll have a look at it tomorrow morning," Thorn said. Thinking to himself, *for all the good that it will do.*

He knew enough about shipbuilding and mechanics to

recite how steamboats operated but collision damage could be difficult to analyze, even with special training Thorn did not possess. Between viewing the ship and speaking to its ex-first mate—if Travis would consent to meet him—Gideon hoped to create a picture in his mind of what had happened to the *Faust*.

And there was still its owner, Armond Joslin, who might well have insights of his own.

"I hate to nag you," Kenfield said, intruding on Thorn's reverie. "About that interview..."

"I had a big lunch and I'm skipping supper," Thorn said, "but I wouldn't mind a drink or three. Are you stuck here, or can you steal some time away?"

"For this, I'll make time," Kenfield told him, smiling. "I foresee a headline coming up on Friday."

"Not sure that I rate the ink," said Gideon, "but you're the editor."

"And publisher," Kenfield replied. "*And* sole reporter. I can guarantee you won't be crowded out, unless we get a monster crawling through the streets and snatching people off the sidewalks."

After Texas and some of the other jobs he'd handled since then, Gideon wasn't prepared to rule out any such event, saying that aloud would only prod the *Independent*'s owner into more sensational verbiage. If Thorn could not prevent publicity, at least he could do everything within his power to ensure that whatever Kenfield published on Friday would be factual, without too many side trips into florid speculation.

"Do you have someplace in town you like to go?" Thorn asked.

"I normally stop off for day's end at the Brass Rail Tavern, one block south on Franklin Street. Boatmen mostly stick to dives along the waterfront, so there's no brawling—well, not much—and Eddie's fancy women are as close as Natchez has to being upper crust."

"Who's Eddie?"

"Last name's Cothran. He's the Rail's proprietor, a member of the city council, supposedly he studies law, although I've never seen a license hanging in the bar."

"Helps if he's sued for anything, I guess," Thorn said.

"Just let me grab my jacket and a notebook, if you will," Kenfield replied.

"No rush on my account."

When he returned from the backroom, Kenfield had doffed his green eyeshade, replaced it with a bowler hat, and donned a jacket. Whether he'd removed the garters from his sleeves, Thorn couldn't tell.

They left the office, Kenfield lingering to lock the red door after them, then glanced across the street and waved at someone standing over there. Gideon tracked his gaze and saw a uniformed policeman leaning up against a brick wall at an alley's mouth, lifting his chin as an acknowledgement of Jubal's greeting.

"You get on all right with beat cops," Thorn observed.

"I try to," Kenfield granted. "But that isn't a patrolman."

"Oh?"

"Chief of police," the newsman said. "Name's Hal Hightower."

"Chief," Thorn echoed. "And does he often watch your office?"

"I suspect he watches everything," Kenfield replied. "Now, how about that drink or three?"

THREE

THE BRASS RAIL TAVERN

Entering the barroom, Jubal Kenfield close behind him, Thorn experienced the same reaction he'd encountered earlier at Pepper Jack's, but amplified by alcohol the tavern's patrons had consumed.

Most conversation stuttered, stalled, and then resumed in softer tones as Gideon and Kenfield stepped up to an open section of the bar and ordered mugs of beer. Some drinkers greeted Jubal but Thorn guessed their welcomes would have seemed more earnest if the *Independent*'s publisher had come alone.

Thorn paid the bartender and tipped him, then steered Kenfield toward an empty table on the south side of the barroom, far enough removed from other seated customers and poker players to confound eavesdropping. Background music from an old player piano helped to keep their conversation private.

Kenfield set a small notepad beside his mug, withdrew a sharpened pencil from an inside pocket of his coat, and opened with, "I understand, from what I've read, that your pursuit of mysteries around the country stems from private tragedy?"

Thorn sipped his beer, considered how to answer that, then gave the short version of how his family had been annihilated back in 1854. The story had been told before in print, by Dinah Pilcher and by other editors who mostly got it right, and Thorn refrained from going into any gory details that he still recalled.

Aside from shortening the interview, he didn't want to step on anything that Dinah might intend to publish if she ever got around to finishing the book she'd planned to write about his life. Last time they spoke, before the Arkansas nightmare, she hadn't settled on a title for it but was leaning toward *Ghost Rider,* which he thought was both melodramatic and inaccurate.

So far, only one of the jobs he'd undertaken had to do with ghosts, and that would be one of the hardest stories to support with facts.

When Gideon was finished with his childhood reminiscence, Kenfield followed up with reference to how he'd solved his childhood mystery. "But after many years," the newsman said, "you finally discovered what had been responsible. Is that right?"

"Not so many years, I guess," Thorn said, "depending on your point of view. I'd hate for anyone to think I'm in my dotage."

"Obviously not," Jubal agreed. "But you *did* catch up to the creature responsible in Colorado Territory, now the thirty-eighth state of the Union since last August?"

"I caught up with *something,*" Thorn replied, "and I *believe* it was the creature from before. A bear can live that long with luck, from what I learned at Harvard."

"Was it *just* a bear, though?" Kenfield prodded.

"Last I heard, biologists at CAC still hadn't narrowed down the species. By the time they got ahold of it, there wasn't that much left, you understand."

"CAC?"

"Colorado Agricultural College."

"Ah. But they have *some* idea by now?" Jubal replied.

Thorn shrugged and said, "I haven't kept in touch with them of late."

That was the truth, but only part of it. He'd paid for an examination of the beast's remains and still expected a report, but when he'd last communicated with Professor Herschel Goins, the department chairman, his people were divided between calling it a mutant grizzly or a relict cave bear, presumed extinct since sometime in the Pleistocene—or last Ice Age—with fossils previously limited to the Old World, ranging from Britain eastward into Russia.

Whether he would ever know the truth or not was still an open question.

"Well, I hope you'll keep in touch and let my readers know what you find out," said Kenfield.

"If I can," Thorn said. Thinking, *if either one of us is still around.*

A figure pushing through The Brass Rail's swinging doors distracted Gideon. Keeping his poker face intact, he nodded toward the entrance, saying, "There's your chief again. Is this part of his normal rounds?"

"You never know with Hal," Jubal replied, raising a hand toward Hightower, who managed not to notice him.

"He's got no normal working hours?" Thorn inquired.

"Not so you'd notice," Kenfield answered. "Lives alone and never married from the background information I've collected. Some might say the job's his life."

"And is he any good at it?" Gideon asked.

"He keeps the peace," Jubal replied. "Or, anyway, as much of it as anybody could, trying to keep the lid on in a Mississippi river town."

Thorn watched Chief Hightower approach the bar, decline an offered drink and start a conversation with the bearded bartender. Five seconds into it, the barkeep glanced over toward Thorn and Kenfield, whereupon the chief hissed something at him and the younger man's cheeks reddened with embarrassment.

Missing the publisher's next question, Thorn was busy hoping that the chief would not become an obstacle to his investigation in Natchez.

But if he did, then Gideon would have to find a way around him and proceed.

"Talking to Jubal Kenfield," Grover Arquette said, as if the observation left a bad taste in his mouth.

"As thick as thieves, I'd say," Chief Hightower replied.

He had been hesitant to pester Arquette at his home on Homochitto Street, but since the Democratic Party leader had instructed him to shadow Thorn, there'd seemed to be no way around it.

"That could be a problem," said Arquette.

"How's that, sir?" Hightower inquired.

"Because the man travels around disturbing towns like ours, Hal. Pokes his nose in where it don't belong and isn't wanted, if you follow me."

Hightower didn't feel like pleading ignorance. Instead, he took a shot and asked, "You mean about the *Faust*, sir?"

"And the foolish talk about a monster living in the

river," Arquette said, scowling. "Who in his right mind would believe that kind of shit?"

"It beats me, sir."

Hightower wasn't sure about those tales himself but wouldn't contradict the man who could dismiss him with a word and run his ass out of the county as an afterthought. The chief adored his badge and the authority that came along with it. He wasn't giving all that up to argue about whether there were big snakes swimming in the Mississippi.

"You know the trouble that could cause for us."

Arquette was clearly stating that as face, and Chief Hightower felt obliged to go along with him, say, "Yes, sir."

Not strictly true, and Arquette didn't seem to be convinced, launching into a speech he meant to prove his point.

"For one thing," he began, "it stands to cost our city money."

"How's that, sir?"

"Why, just imagine it! Suppose the men in charge of shipping lines decide it isn't safe to stop at Natchez for their pickups and deliveries. How long do you suppose the shops could stay in business, waiting for their goods to reach them overland?"

"I never thought about it, sir," the chief said truthfully.

"Well, think about it now, Hal. And imagine what would happen to the service industries—the restaurants, hotels, saloons, the gambling halls, even the whorehouses —if travelers stop coming here on riverboats. The city could dry up and blow away, by God!"

Hightower reckoned that Arquette was going overboard but didn't plan to say so. Rather, he replied as was expected of him, simply saying, "Yes, sir."

"And then, you've got the niggers," said Arquette, dropping his voice an octave as he spoke the too-familiar racial slur that passed for common speech in the Magnolia State and all across the South.

"Sir?"

Hightower was well acquainted with his race's fear of colored folk and understood a big part of his job was keeping them in line, restricted to what whites regarded as "their place," but how that came together with a river monster sinking paddle boats eluded him.

"Just think about it, Chief," Arquette admonished Hightower. "They're ignorant and superstitious, barely one step from the jungle, and they hate us for the fact of our superiority. Ain't that the blessed truth?"

Hightower nodded on command. He couldn't very well deny that former slaves were short on education, since state law had banned it until 1865 and vigilantes from the Ku Klux Klan had waged a war on northern radicals who tried to make up that deficiency during the Reconstruction years. As for the shibboleth of white supremacy, Hightower never doubted it and did his best to see its rigid code observed, but when he thought about some of the sorry white folks he encountered through his job—the shiftless drunkards, wife-and-child-beaters, inbred sluggards who would rather starve than do an hour's honest work—he wondered how they could be rated as superior to anyone or anything.

"You think they'd cause some devilment?" he asked Arquette, almost forgetting to add "sir."

"Just think about it, Chief. They worshipped animals in Africa, you know?"

"I might've heard something about it, sir."

"So, if they think a giant snake's prowling around and

sinking white men's ships, what's stopping them from calling it a sign? If it's a message from one of their pagan gods, couldn't their preachers tell 'em it's a message to rise up and kill us in our beds? What happens to our women then, Chief?"

It surprised Hightower to discover he'd started heating up a bit himself, hearing the same speech that he'd listened to a thousand times before, now with a serpent god tossed in.

"What should we do, sir?" he inquired.

"What *you* should do is have a word with Yancy Olson. Maybe have him and his boys discourage this Thorn character from feeling too at home, asking too many goddamned questions."

"I can do that, sir."

"I know you can," Arquette said with a smile. "It's for the good of Natchez, after all."

Gideon's pocket watch read 8:16 p.m. when he entered the Haverstock Hilltop hotel. He didn't recognize the clerk on duty but assumed it must be Hub Ingram, described to him that early afternoon.

The clerk's name tag read "HUBERT," which explained the nickname. Thorn had wondered what possessed a parent who would name a child after the center of a wheel but knew it wouldn't be the strangest given name he had encountered in his travels—or at Harvard, come to that.

Gideon introduced himself Ingram, got a smile and handshake in return, determining that no messages had been left for him during his absence. He had not expected one, and knew from long experience that when he worked a special job, no news was often for the best.

Upstairs, Thorn checked his room for any signs of tampering while he was out, found none, and locked himself inside. For good measure, he took the single straight-backed chair and wedged it underneath the doorknob as an extra level of security.

He had no reason to expect that anybody might burst in upon him through the night, but Gideon had been surprised before and learned from his mistakes. Tonight, the knowledge that Natchez's top policeman was collecting information on him, with no clear-cut goal in mind, encouraged Thorn to keep his guard up, draw the curtains on his bedroom's single window, turning down the room's gas lamps to minimize shadows tracking across the drapes.

That done, he stripped and washed up in the water closet, then prepared for bed. Checking his weapons was the next priority and didn't take much time. His twin Colts and his lever-action rifle were all loaded with .44-40 Winchester rounds, so called for pairing .44-caliber lead projectiles with forty grains of black powder per cartridge. The net result was a fourteen-gram bullet traveling 1,245 feet per second with a maximum effective range around one hundred feet for pistols, out to 125 yards from the rifle's twenty-four-inch barrel.

As for the big Sharps, it was never loaded unless Thorn had reason to unwrap if from its buckskin sheath and aim it for a long shot at a target otherwise beyond his range.

When Thorn turned in, he let his gun belt curled beside him with the hammer thongs unhooked for easy drawing if he had to do it half asleep. He didn't think he'd need the Bowie knife but liked to have it handy, just in case. His Winchester stood at his bedside, muzzle pointed toward the ceiling, but he'd left its firing chamber empty, reckoning that if he couldn't stop intruders with his first twelve pistol shots, the rifle wouldn't be much use to him.

While drifting off to sleep, he thought about tomorrow's plans. The first thing after breakfast he would go to see the *Faust*'s wreckage, before another day passed and an unofficial salvage crew could go to work with axes. Moving on from there, he'd try to have a quiet word with Purnell Travis, lone survivor of the steamer's grim demise.

And fading out, Thorn hoped he would not dream.

CEMETERY ROAD, NATCHEZ

"We heard about that Yankee, Chief."

"Heard what, exactly," Hal Hightower asked.

"Just what I said. A goddamn Yankee, down from somewhere in New England thereabouts," Yancy Olson replied, and spat murky tobacco juice off the front porch of his dilapidated shanty house.

"That's all?" the chief pressed him.

"What else you need? Seems like we ain't got rid a all the carpetbaggers yet."

"Uh-huh. Here's what we need from you," Hightower said, "and this comes from the top."

He didn't need to tell Olson who was on top in Natchez. If they didn't have a visit coming up from Governor John Stone or one of Mississippi's U.S. senators—Blanche Bruce or James Z. George—that label only fit one man that Yancy knew about.

And come to think of it, there wouldn't be a celebration if Bruce came to town, unless it was a necktie party for the ex-slave who had wormed his way into the Senate two years earlier, now courting a high-yellow woman out of

Philadelphia by way of Cleveland in Ohio (not the one in southeast Mississippi's Bolivar County).

Olson's whitecaps would love to get their hands on Bruce, no doubt about it, and his dwindling bunch of friends in Washington be damned.

Today, the man on top in Natchez was Grover Arquette, an Adams County planter who had once owned some four hundred slaves and spent the war in the Confederate States Congress while Olson and other poor white trash were dying by the thousands in defense of hearth, home, and white womanhood. Over the past two years, since white rule was restored in Mississippi, followed by the rigged election of President Rutherford B. Hayes—who'd made a deal with former leaders of the Klan to pull any remaining occupation troops out of the conquered South, except where they were needed to keep killing red men—Arquette was the one and only kingmaker in Adams and its three adjoining counties, Franklin, Jefferson, and Wilkinson.

"First thing," Hightower said, in answer to his question, "you-all are required to keep an eye on this Gideon Thorn. Can't miss 'im, dressed up all in black and wearing two Colts on his belt."

"He any good with 'em?" asked Yancy.

"How 'n Hell would I know that?"

"Don't matter," Olson answered. Thinking to himself that it could damn well matter if their spying on the stranger turned to shooting, but he kept that morsel to himself. "What else?"

"See where he goes and who he talks to, but be sly about it, yeah? Don't show up in a robe, waving a Rebel flag."

"We can do that."

"And tell me what he's up to," said the town's police

chief. "I can pass it on and get back to you if he needs discouraging."

"Or maybe disappearing?" Olson queried, hopefully.

He missed the good old Reconstruction days of riding out at night in full Ku Klux regalia, raiding darkies' shacks, torching their churches and their schools. The modern whitecaps were all right, far as they went, but Yancy doubted they would ever hold a candle to the Klan.

"Don't overstep your bounds," Hightower cautioned him, stern-faced. "Remember you be takin' orders and not givin' 'em."

"No problem," Olson said, and flashed the chief a crooked smile that nobody with half a brain would ever trust.

OFFSHORE FROM VIDALIA, LOUISIANA

Residents along the Mississippi, whether living on the east bank or the west, judged that their states had title to the river halfway out from shore, split down the middle by a line no one could see and only surveyors armed with cosmolabes, dioptra and theodolites could calculate.

For most, dead reckoning was good enough, particularly after nightfall, when the river ran as black as printer's ink.

Vidalia natives Lucius Reeves and Alvy Lauber, trolling after catfish underneath a half moon, well past midnight Thursday, June twenty-first, had first-rate reasons for beginning their excursion while most decent people were asleep.

First, neither Lauber nor Reeves possessed a fishing license, which had never bothered them before and likely wouldn't get them into trouble now, so long as they could claim they hooked their catch beyond the river's midpoint, on the Mississippi side. Game wardens rarely worked this late and didn't care much about catfish anyhow, regarding them as bottom-feeding scavengers on par with skunks and weasels, though much better eating when fileted and fried.

Second, and by far the more important, was a reason that fell on the social side of judgment's scale. Alvy Lauber was white, while Lucius Reeves was black, a former slave.

Under Louisiana law—and Mississippi's too, hell, damn near everyplace across the late Confederacy—whites and blacks were meant to live apart, except where white employers and their overseers worked black laborer in an approximation of their antebellum roles. Oh, sure, the blacks received a pittance for their work these days, often in trade as sharecroppers, but most were bound by labor contracts to their former masters or descendants of them, subject to imprisonment if they walked off a job without written permission from their white employers.

And if jailed for that offense, they wound up working for the state at zero wages till their time was up, assuming it crossed some white warden's mind to turn them loose. At which point, it was understood they'd go back to the boss they had deserted in the first place, first apologizing (tears preferred), then settling for an even lower wage than they'd run off from the last time.

Lauber and Reeves had grown up to the age when parents separated children based on color, sending some to work the fields or clean some Anglo Saxon lady's house, the rest—white kids—scrounging for jobs if they were boys, the girls hunting for husbands who would put them on a pedestal at home, then sneak out for brown sugar after sundown.

Staying friendly as adults, particularly in Louisiana,

where some eighteen hundred ex-slaves had been executed for the "crime" of casting ballots back in 1868, ranked high on any list of truly terrible ideas. The only thing that former Kluxers—many of them "whitecaps" now and still night-riding when they got a chance—despised more than a Negro was a white man they had marked down as a "nigger-lover."

Short of fiddling around with someone's sister, then ignoring her when she turned up with child, race-mixing was the quickest way in postwar Dixie to court sudden death.

"You brought the shad guts and the nightcrawlers?" Reeves asked his secret friend of twenty years.

"Didn't I show 'em to you?" Lauber answered back.

"Just makin' sure is all," Reeves said.

"Help me start baitin' up these lines and get 'em in the water, will you? I don't wanna float around out here all night."

"You still skittish about dem big ole snakes?" Reeves teased.

"Skittish my ass. Katie's talkin' about another baby if you can believe it, and I gotta do my bit or never hear the end of it."

"Hey, if you need a hand with that..."

"Don't let them whitecaps hear you joke about it," Lauber cautioned.

"Who said I was jokin'?"

"Makes it even worse," Lauber replied, but he was smiling through the mock anger.

Once they had dropped their lines into the water, the allowed the skiff to float downstream a mile or so. When it had reached that point, they'd take turns on the oars and bring it back on point, midway between the scattered lights of Vidalia and brighter glow from Natchez, showing off the district where drinking and whoring went on until nearly dawn.

Reeves got the first bite on one of his lines and started pulling in the catch. "Feels like a good-sized 'un," he said.

"Better be, if I'm trying to pop another ankle-biter out."

Lucius still had approximately half the line to go when both men felt an unexpected swell beneath their skiff, raising it two or three feet easily before it settled back."

"The hell was that?" asked Lauber.

"Got no idea," Reeves said. Then, half a second later, "Shit! My line's gone slack!"

He hauled it in, hand over hand, and held its cut end up for Lauber to observe by moonlight.

"Catfish bit through it," Lauber proposed.

"Did no such thing, Alvy. This wasn't gnawed through. It was cut off clean."

"By what?"

"You're askin' me? Maybe a gator."

"Wasn't any gator made that swell we felt."

And then, as if his words had conjured repetition of the former surge in current, Lauber felt the skiff rising again. This time, instead of two or three feet, it kept going—four, five, nearly six—until he felt the light craft balanced on some solid object underneath it, tipping to the left and going over in a death roll.

Alvy Lauber had no chance to cry out in alarm before the river pitch-black river swallowed him alive.

FOUR

PEPPER JACK'S STEAK HOUSE

From his hotel window, Gideon observed the restaurant put out its "OPEN" sign for early breakfast customers and took a window seat ten minutes later, noting only three more tables occupied. He didn't recognize the diners from his visit yesterday and guessed that they were Natchez merchants stoking up before another long day peddling their wares to Thursday shoppers.

Jacque Beauchamp's waitress on the morning shift wasn't the same one he'd encountered yesterday—brunette instead of blond, older and wearing wire-rimmed spectacles—but she was affable and didn't stare when Gideon removed his hat.

He ordered Cajun scrambled eggs spiced up with garlic and hot sauce, plus Andouille sausage on the side with mushrooms and thick buttered toast. Chicory coffee rounded off the meal, which Thorn enjoyed at leisure, watching pedestrians and horseback riders start to circulate on Silver Street. A few showed signs of late-night celebration in the Trace City's saloons, but most seemed wide and ready to confront another day.

Thorn got along without a visit from the chef this morning, thankful for that small degree of solitude as other tables filled around him, new arrivals flicking glances toward him while they settled down to order food. Gideon wondered whether any of them knew his business in their city, but the *Independent*'s interview would not appear until tomorrow morning.

Even so...

Finished, Thorn paid his tab and left a dollar for the waitress, knowing it would likely strike her as extravagant. Outside, he walked back to his hotel's stable and found Kelsey Underhill already on the job, pleased to accept a dollar bill for standing back while Gideon exchanged some quiet thoughts with Bell and Shadow, then saddled the stallion on his own.

Jubal Kenfield had given him directions to the site upstream where he could view the *Faust*'s mortal remains. No trace of any crewmen other than the paddle steamer's sole survivor had been found so far, ten days after what Kenfield called "the incident," and residents familiar with the mighty Mississippi doubted they would ever surface now.

The river, vast and strong, routinely swept away its victims, animal and human, sending them downstream to Baton Rouge or past it, to the Gulf of Mexico, unless a hungry alligator snatched one or an eddy drove the sodden corpse into a cove. Riding along the river's western bank, Thorn marveled at its size and power, irresistible at flood tide, driving all before it to oblivion.

There's been a time, as he had learned in school, when a series of powerful earthquakes had rocked Missouri, centered on the town of New Madrid, their tremors felt as far away as Boston, where they ran church bells. The shocks were spaced over a three-month period, causing the Mississippi to flow backwards in a fluvial tsunami, creating new waterfalls in an instant and dashing at least thirty boats to their doom with all hands. The aftershocks collapsed brick walls in Cincinnati, woke America's First Lady at the White House, dug new lakes in Arkansas and Tennessee, killing more than one thousand people overall.

But all of that had happened between mid-December of 1811 and early March in 1812. Since then, most of the great catastrophe's survivors had had expired, their remnant further decimated by the Civil War, and memories had faded.

Until now, when the immutable Father of Waters struck again, albeit on a smaller scale.

Thorn found the *Faust* upriver, where Kenfield had pointed him, capsized and jammed into the Mississippi's western shore, anchored by its inverted smokestacks in deep mud. He didn't try to board the vessel, foiled by overhanging trees and creaking sounds suggesting that the river might reclaim its prize at any moment, even after leaving it at rest so long.

In fact, he didn't need to board the *Faust* or ask for anyone's opinion of the paddle steamer's fate. Its hull had been torn open near the keel, as if a jagged boulder had arisen from the river's depths, gutting the ship in much the same way that a fisherman would clean his catch. From what he saw, it was impossible to say exactly *what* had cleaved those timbers with so much destructive force, but if he squinted just right at the wreckage, Thorn imagined that he could see tooth or claw marks on some of the shattered beams.

Ridiculous?

Gideon couldn't say, but knew his next stop had to be a visit with the only man who'd managed to escape the *Faust* alive.

Yancy Olson hung well back while following Gideon Thorn north from Natchez. The whitecap leader held his varnish Appaloosa to a walk, knowing the man in black could not elude him without deviating from the Mississippi's course and striking off into the woods.

Not likely. And, in fact, he had a pretty good idea where Thorn was headed after breakfasting at Pepper Jack's.

Is he was interested in wild stories of the river monster, what else could have drawn him out this way except the paddle steamer *Faust*'s washed-up remains?

"Fat lotta good seeing that wreck will do 'im," Yancy told his gelding as they clopped along.

The horse made no reply.

Olson was following Chief Hightower's instructions to the letter—follow Thorn around and then report on his itinerary—with no plan of facing off against the Yankee bastard.

Not yet, anyhow.

Which didn't mean that Yancy hadn't come prepared for trouble, just in case.

The holster on his left hip, situated for a cross-hand draw, was heavy with a Colt Model 1861 Navy revolver weighing two and a half pounds, chambered for .38-caliber centerfire cartridges. On his right hip, Olson wore a sheathed Arkansas toothpick, a variation on the classic Bowie knife whose twenty-inch double-edged blade made it the next best thing to a sword.

Yancy had carried both the knife and pistol during wartime, as a member of Mississippi's 11th Consolidated Cavalry, and he'd brought them home with him after Appomattox, wielding them in defense of the white race through Reconstruction and beyond.

In fact, he had begun to think the war might never end.

This morning, Yancy sat and watched from hiding as the black-clad Massachusetts interloper eyeballed the *Faust*, or what was left of it. Wisely, he didn't try to board the capsized ship, though Olson would have gladly watched him try it, laughing while he drowned. When Thorn returned from staring at the wreck to mount his stallion once again, Yancy had found a new place of concealment, ready to resume pursuit.

Asking himself, *Where's the damned Yankee going now?*

Unless he'd pulled up stakes and moved since yesterday, Thorn trusted Jubal Kenfield's word that he could find survivor Purnell Travis dwelling on the northern outskirts of Natchez. The former first mate's home turned out to be a shotgun house a quarter mile outside of town, with no neighbors in sight.

Shotgun houses tended to be small, rectangular, their rooms constructed one behind the other, with a door at either end. The name derived from supposition that a shotgun could be fired through one door or the other, its projectiles passing down a central corridor and exiting without striking the walls on either side.

The hovel that he'd found by following directions from the *Independent*'s publisher needed a coat of fresh paint and new shingles on its sloping roof. One of the two windows in front was broken, missing glass replaced with tar paper tacked to the outer frame. The front door, badly warped, would barely close, and weeds had overgrown what someone likely once intended as a lawn.

Thorn tried to place the smell that emanated from the shack, deciding that it was a rank mélange of cooking grease, mildew and rotting wood. Shadow recoiled from the effluvium until Thorn made a silent promise that the stallion wouldn't have to go inside.

Gideon didn't relish the thought himself, but since he'd come this far...

Dismounting, he approached the warped front door and knocked, watching it shiver in its frame from the impact. He waited for a moment, was about to try again, when he heard shuffling footsteps from inside and the door opened to reveal a balding man of average stature and build, gin blossoms coloring his bulbous nose a ripe magenta hue.

Squinting, the shanty's occupant asked, "Who 'n hell are you?"

Thorn answered with a query of his own. "Purnell Travis?"

"Who's asking?"

Thorn identified himself and asked if Travis would be willing to discuss the *Faust*'s demise.

"I got enough dumb bastards laughing at me as it is. Don't need another one from up in Yankee Land."

"That's not my aim, sir. I'm just looking for the truth about what happened ten days back."

"Who sent you?" Travis challenged him.

"No one. I'm here on my own time and at my own expense. If you know something that can spare more people from whatever happened to your crew, I hope you'll share it with me for the sake of future victims."

Travis squinted at him, frowning, straightening a bit before he asked, "You swear to that?"

"I do," Thorn said.

Another minute crept away, then Travis said, "All right, then. If you reckon you can stop it, come on in."

The little house smelled even worse inside. Thorn compensated, breathing through his mouth, declining his host's offer of a seat on mossy-looking furniture.

"Whiskey?" asked Travis.

"No, thanks. But you go ahead."

"Don't need permission underneath my own roof, do I?" Shuffling to the kitchen for a nearly empty bottle, he returned and said, "Go on and ask your questions, then."

"I'd like to start with what you saw that night," Gideon said.

Travis drank from his bottle, grimaced, and replied, "I couldn't see much, with the dark that night and all, but I *can* tell you it was like nothing I ever saw before and never hope to see again. It was the first thing since I was a little shaver that made me believe in Hell."

"If you could be a little more specific..."

"It was a goddamn giant monster," Travis asked. "No other word for it, all right? Now go ahead and laugh if you've a mind to. I've got used to it."

Yancy Olson grew restless after forty minutes watching from the woods near the old shanty Purnell Travis occupied. He hadn't known who had the place at first, but recognized the river boatman when he opened up his door.

It took a bit of time for Thorn to talk his way inside, then Travis shut the door as best he could and Olson reckoned he could only eavesdrop on their conversation if he crept up on the house and maybe found a window opened to relieve the pent-up heat inside.

Fat chance that he was risking that and maybe getting picked off for his trouble.

Helping Chief Hightower out was one thing. Getting killed on his behalf was something else entirely.

Yancy checked his tarnished pocket watch each time he started getting antsy, conscious of time slipping through his fingers. If he went back to the chief with nothing to report beyond Thorn's movements, Hightower was going to be irritated with him, at the very least. If he got mad at Olson, that could influence Grover Arquette, and if Arquette should turn against him...

Well, the whitecap leader couldn't stand for that.

Considering his options, Yancy thought that he could bushwhack Thorn before they made it back to Natchez. That might solve the problem, or it might rebound against Olson if the chief took umbrage against him showing initiative.

The men in charge of Natchez—meaning *white* men—didn't like their redneck lackeys thinking for themselves and running off on tangents like a bunch of chickens with their heads lopped off. In fact, exceeding orders was the quickest way that Yancy Olson knew to get his head cut off—or other body parts he wouldn't like to do without.

The best thing, Olson finally decided, was to leave off wasting watching a rundown shack and head on back to town. He would report to Hightower what he had seen and leave the theorizing to his betters.

Unlike white scalawags who'd proved themselves disloyal to Mother Dixie, and the darkies who would grab for anything within their reach unless restrained, Yancy Olson knew his place. He was a southern patriot, by God, and no one could take that away from him while he was drawing breath.

The trick now was to keep on breathing, being useful to the Power That Be, but not be trodden underfoot.

With that in mind, still sorting out the details, Olson climbed aboard his varnish Appaloosa gelding, turned it back toward town, and urged it to a gallop heading homeward.

Would this turn out to be a blockhead move?

He didn't know for sure and wouldn't until he was face to face with Hightower, at which point it would be too late to change his mind. But if he played it up as hazardous, exaggerated his concern over the risk of being spotted as he followed Thorn, it just might sell.

And if his luck held out, the news of Thorn interrogating Purnell Travis ought to spur Mr. Arquette and Chief Hightower toward eliminating any human risks.

That kind of clean-up was a job that Yancy Olson knew only too well.

He had no feelings about Travis one way or another, just a drunk who ran his mouth too much. But any time he got to kill a Yankee—even now, a dozen years beyond the war—Olson was loath to let it pass.

In fact, he just might do that on his own, whether the men standing above him on the Natchez social ladder gave the word or not.

Gideon had a lot to think about while he was riding back to town.

For starters, there was Purnell Travis's description of the creature he had seen ten nights ago. Granting that it was dark, considering the first mate's taste for alcohol, his story still rang true to Thorn. He figured Travis must have seen *something,* although he couldn't pin it down and most of the details were vague.

Travis insisted that he'd seen a "monster," at least roughly serpentine in form, although he couldn't say if it had fins or legs. He estimated that the thing had been a trifle longer than the *Faust*, call it sixty feet or so, but that likely owed something to the night, Travis's fear, and long wakes generated by the steamer and its enemy.

Most people had trouble judging a trout's length seeing it in clear, calm water, much less animals they'd never seen before under deceptive, harsh conditions. Strangers to the woods might see a fawn and take it for a full-grown moose or make a barn cat out to be a mountain lion. Estimating any snake's length while it wriggled, coiled and struck could be particularly problematic—even more so underwater and at night. How many people watched a bird in flight, mistaking both its wingspan and its altitude?

Against those arguments, Thorn had his observation of the *Faust* and its condition when it washed ashore. He also had his sense that Purnell Travis only told his story as he did today, despite ten days of public ridicule, because he took it for the truth.

Who else might Thorn consult?

Only one answer came to mind.

Arriving back in town, Thorn rode directly to the *Natchez Independent*'s office and found Jubal Kenfield busy in the backroom, as he had been yesterday. The tinkling doorbell brought Kenfield out front, smiling at sight of Thorn and asking, "May I ask you how it went?"

"It went," Gideon said, without elaborating. "Can you see your way clear to another favor for me, if it doesn't cramp your style too much in town?"

"I'd have to hear the favor."

"Something Purnell Travis mentioned," Gideon replied. "I can't be too specific now, but it might help if I could talk to Mr. Joslin from the Natchez & New Orleans Line."

The newsman blinked at that, then said, "And that would be because...?"

"I can't get into it without verification," Thorn said. "If I manage that and get some mileage out of it, the story's yours as soon as it's resolved."

"Exclusively?"

"I haven't stumbled on another publisher in town so far."

"Joslin's a busy man, as you may well imagine," Kenfield said, frowning. "I've interviewed him briefly, but I wouldn't call us peers by any means."

"Still, you could ask him?"

"I can get a message to him through his private secretary, Margaret Duchamp. She'll pass it on to him; I'm sure of that. Whether he'll answer me or not, I couldn't promise you."

"But maybe if you worded it to pique his interest?"

"Saying what, specifically?"

"You have a pencil handy?"

"Mr. Thorn, this *is* a newsroom," Kenfield said, raising a hand to feel behind one ear, then blushing when he found no pencil there. "Just wait a second, please."

He ducked into the backroom once again, returning with a freshly sharpened pencil and a notepad that he settled on the outer office counter.

"All set. Fire when ready."

Thorn chose his words carefully, striving for brevity with punch behind it. Kenfield wrote it word-for-word, raising his head when he was done to ask, "You're serious about this?"

"Never more so," Gideon assured him.

"But..."

"Look at it this way," Thorn continued. "If I'm right, whichever way it goes, you'll have the story of the year, maybe for any year since printing was invented."

"And if you're mistaken?"

"You've still got a front-page story, telling everyone how Joslin laughed me out of town."

The newsman nodded. Said, "Your funeral, I guess."

Thorn forced a smile. Replied, "We'll have to wait and see on that."

FIVE

NATCHEZ & NEW ORLEANS LINE HEADQUARTERS

Armond Joslin was fifty-five years old and looked it. Although reasonably fit and seldom seen without a tailored three-piece suit and highly polished shoes, he had not found a way to mask the baggy pouches underneath his pale gray eyes or the dewlap underneath his chin which stubbornly defied stiff detachable collars and bowties.

Facing the black-clad stranger seated in his office, barely half his own age, Joslin felt at something of a disadvantage, never mind his spacious desk, the paintings on his office walls, or all the money he'd accumulated in his several bank accounts.

Feeling an unaccustomed need to put the young man in his place, he said, "I am a busy man, as you may well imagine."

"Yes, sir. And I thank you for your time," Gideon Thorn replied.

Before this meeting, Joslin had dispatched a telegram to

Boston and had been surprised to learn that Thorn, for all his youth and rumored strange ideas about the world, Thor rivaled Joslin's affluence and had, in fact, surpassed it several times over.

Granted, that was mostly down to his forebears, but still...

"You're only sitting here," Joslin pressed on, "because I'm fond of Jubal Kenfield and he's done my company some valuable favors in the past." That said, he felt constrained to add, "And your short note intrigued me."

Thorn said nothing in reply to that but held the shipping magnate's steady gaze. Slightly unsettled, Joslin raised the piece of folded-over foolscap paper from his desktop, opened it, and read its brief message aloud.

"You write, 'The *Faust* was not your first loss.' How on Earth would you know that, sir?"

"Purnell Travis," Thorn replied, and left it there.

Joslin allowed himself a weary sigh. "That one? I see. You understand the mental trauma that he's suffered, being sole survivor of the recent tragedy? No doubt, if you've been to the shanty that he calls a home, you've also seen him taking refuge in a whiskey bottle."

Thorn dismissed that with a gesture of his right hand. Asked, "So, was he lying to me, Mr. Joslin? When he spoke about the other boats you've lost this year, I mean?"

"Who are you to come here and interrupt my working day with accusations?"

"It's a question, not an accusation," Thorn replied. "And since you're ducking it, I have my answer."

"I could have you thrown out on the street," Joslin blustered. "I could request that our police chief see you out of Natchez, sir."

"You're only two-thirds right on that score, Mr. Joslin.

You can ban me from your office, certainly. I won't resist if that's your pleasure. And you can *request* Chief Hightower to run me out of town, but we both know he has no legal right or cause for that. One telegram to Block, Enright & Sloan in Boston and you'll find yourself tied up in court for months, explaining why you think so little of the U.S. Constitution."

Bristling, Joslin told his visitor, "I might remind you this is Mississippi, sir."

"And some folks living here still think they won the War Between the States," said Thorn. "Forgive me if I don't mistake you for a fool."

Joslin wished for a stiff whiskey but couldn't bring himself to fetch a bottle from his office sideboard, much less offer Thorn the taste that common courtesy would then require. After a moment wasted glowering across his desk, Joslin reluctantly admitted, "Very well, then. Mr. Travis is correct. I've lost two other vessels on the river in the past few months. One was a livestock barge. Neither the pilot, his two crewmen, nor the animals survived."

"Were any of them found?" Thorn asked.

"Few victims of the Mississippi are. It takes a fluke for man or beast to snag on roots along the shoreline or slip into coves."

"And what about the other boat?"

"Transporting cotton to St. Louis. Of four men aboard her, three survived."

"And told you what?" Thorn pressed.

"Some fantasy about a dragon, as they called it. Not the flying sort, mind you, but swimming like some giant eel or snake."

Thorn frowned. Said, "Eel. I hadn't thought of that."

"What *are* you thinking?"

The intruder answered with a question of his own. "I take for granted that you've checked up on me?"

"If I have?"

"Perhaps you've contacted George Hearst," Thorn said. "He had a problem somewhat like your own two years ago, one of his Texas silver mining operations. I say 'somewhat' because no river was involved, but otherwise the similarities are plain to see."

"George claims he's never heard of you."

"But you know better from the press, I think."

"Suppose that's true. What can you do for me?"

"For best results, we can't be working at cross-purposes," Thorn said. "I'll need more information on your first two losses and whatever else you have to share."

"You haven't heard the news from overnight, across the river?" Joslin asked him.

Frowning, Thorn said, "No. What news?"

"I don't have many details yet," Joslin replied, "but I can point you to someone who might. The thing is..."

"What?"

"You'll have to use discretion if you get in touch with him, or else there could be hell to pay."

Noah Dearborn, president of River City Bank with branches in Vicksburg and Greenville, leaned forward in his high-backed office chair and asked his unexpected visitor, "What did you say this Yankee's name is?"

"You should really try to listen, Noah," Grover Arquette said. "This is important shit I'm telling you."

Dearborn had not expected Arquette's visit on this Thursday afternoon, dragging Chief Hightower along—most certainly had not invited them—but when the district's Democratic Party boss turned up, regardless of the circumstances, savvy businessmen made time for him.

"I understand that, Grover," Dearborn said. "I merely asked you—"

"Thorn. Gideon Thorn, all right?"

"Am I supposed to know him?"

"Read your copy of the *Independent* in the morning. Everyone in Adams County—them that know their letters, anyhow—will know by the time they've finished breakfast."

Dearborn knew damned well that Grover hadn't barged in just to peddle papers. "How about a preview?" he inquired.

"He isn't just some Yankee," said Arquette, "although he *is* from hoity-toity Boston. For a start, he's rich as Croesus, but he doesn't loiter in New England rubbing shoulders with the upper crust and going to cotillions. Not this one."

"All right," Dearborn replied. "I'll bite. What *does* he do, then?"

"He hunts monsters."

Dearborn almost laughed at that, then it sunk in. "Oh, Christ!" he said.

"You bet your ass, 'Oh, Christ!' He's closeted with Armond Joslin right this minute and you know damn well they aren't discussing cotton prices."

Chief Hightower had not spoken yet, but Dearborn swung around to face him now. "How long have you been sitting on this, Hal?" the banker asked.

"He only got in yesterday," the chief replied. "Went to the *Independent* right away, then our with Kenfield after a talk at the Brass Rail."

"About...?" the banker prodded.

Arquette interrupted at that point. "Noah, I've *told* you what he's looking for."

"A monster in the Mississippi?" Dearborn answered back. "Let him look, then. When he doesn't find one, he'll get bored and go away."

"What if he does?" Grover replied.

"Does *what*?" said Dearborn, once again confused.

"Finds one," the party leader said.

"You don't believe that, do you?"

"Doesn't matter what I do or don't believe, Noah. This guy's already working with the *Independent*, and once Jubal runs tomorrow's story, you can bet the *Clarion* will pick it up in Jackson, the *Vicksburg Post*, and how long after that before the *Commercial Appeal* takes a bite at the apple in Memphis. How long after that before we read about it in the *St. Louis Globe-Democrat* or the damn *New York Times*?"

"You might read 'em," said Dearborn. "I won't waste time on fairy tales."

"That's wonderful," Arquette half-sneered at him. "But I don't care what *you* read, Noah. I'm concerned about the customers who'll shy away from doing business on the river if they're feeling skittish, not to mention to mention new investors in the district."

"And the other lunatics who crawl out of the woodwork," Hal Hightower interjected. "They could turn Natchez into a freak show, people laughing at us all across the country and beyond."

"If that's your worry, run this Yankee out of town," Dearborn replied.

"Won't work," Hightower said. "Won't stick. He ain't some two-bit drifter outa nowhere, going no place. Bastard comes from money and he's got a slew of people who believe in him, his wild ideas."

Noah sat back and spread his hands, palms heavenward. "All right, then. What's the answer?"

"First thing," Arquette replied, "is put a lid on Kenfield and the *Independent*."

"He won't let you tell him what to write," Noah objected.

"Maybe not tomorrow morning," said Arquette. "But when his advertisers start to pull their contracts, I suspect he'll reconsider." Turning to Chief Hightower, he added, "In the meantime, keep a close eye on this interloper from New England. Think of some way to discourage him from staying hereabouts."

"Yes, sir." Hightower said. "I know just how to handle it."

"And be damn sure it won't trace back to us."

Cottonwood Road ran through the heart of what some white Natchezians called "Bronzeville," while too many others with their pea brains stuck before the Year of Jubilo branded it "Niggertown."

Erasmus Finch ignored both names, smiling sometimes when he recalled the wartime spiritual that his people sang.

Darkies, can you see the master
With the moustache on his face?
The Yankees come and whip his ass,
He gotta leave this place.
The Yankees come, ha ha!
The master go, ho ho!
And we shall have a jubilation
In the Year of Jubilo!

Finch knew that was supposed to mean the Year of Jubilee, some kind of Jewish thing that came 'round every fifty years or so, supposedly revising ownership of land to make things equitable all around. That hadn't worked out so well for his people since the war, when Union General William Sherman's vow to give each freedman "forty acres and a mule" fell flat and died in Congress, while the Reconstruction-era Klan gave way to Democratic Party "rifle clubs," whitecaps, lynch mobs and chain gangs. Former slaves in Mississippi couldn't vote or sit on juries, could be sent to jail for an "insulting" word or gesture toward their former masters, and were banned from owning guns—although the latter prohibition hadn't bothered Finch so far.

This afternoon, with dusk already coming on, he heard his watchdog yapping at some unexpected visitor's approach. Before he looked to find out who was dropping by, Finch got his double-barreled Greener ten-gauge shotgun from its hiding place, confirmed that it was loaded, and prepared to sell his life dearly.

God knew enough white men in Adams County would have gladly cut it short.

"Who is it?" asked his wife, Caddie.

Erasmus drew the curtain back an inch and felt himself relax. "Just Willem," he replied and set the shotgun down.

Willem Atkins was another freedman, roughly Finch's age, though neither one could rightly date his birth to a specific year. A boatman for the Natchez & New Orleans Line, Willem earned half the pay a white boy would have made for doing the same job, and while he never griped about it to his supervisor, he and Finch had spent many an evening sipping moonshine and comparing miserable lots in life.

He went out to meet Willem, wearing a genuine smile but still checking the tree line for lurkers who might mean his family harm.

"Surprised to see you," he advised Atkins.

"Didn't expect it, neither," Willem said.

"What brings you out, then?"

"Mr. Joslin sent me with a message for you," Willem answered.

"Has it slipped his mind that I ain't on his payroll?"

"Nah. Just wanted me to ask if he can send a white man out to see ya."

That was rich, a white captain of industry asking a black man for permission to do anything.

"Which white man would that be?" Erasmus asked his longtime friend.

"Don't know 'im, but he ain't from anywhere around here."

"Why I wanna see him, then?"

Willem lowered his voice before he answered. "Guess he heard about what happened to your cousin last night."

"Got nothing to do with me," Finch said. "He needs to ask someone across the river, over there in Vidalia."

"I think he wants to talk about that thing. You know."

"Ain't seen it, and I don't know shit about it, just what other people say."

"I get the feeling that he wants to deal with it somehow."

"I ain't a hunting guide, neither," Finch said.

"I hear you. Should I tell the boss that you won't see 'im, then?"

"Hold on, now."

A refusal might be taken as defiance, and Finch didn't want to see what sprang from that.

At last, he said, "I'll see 'im, sure, but I ain't promising to help him find no sea monster."

"He likely won't mind that," Willem replied. "Can't say how anybody else will take it, though."

RIVER CITY BANK

Once Chief Hightower left to run his errand, Grover Arquette lit himself a fat cigar and blew a smoke ring toward the ceiling fan in Noah Dearborn's office.

"Do you think he'll get it done?" the banker asked.

"Chief Hal?" Arquette nodded. "He hasn't let us down before, which is the only reason he's still got that badge."

"Still, with the way you talk about this Yankee—"

"Thorn," Arquette reminded him.

"Whatever. If he's rich and independent like you say, he may not take well to discouragement."

"Depends on how discouraging it gets." Arquette surmised, smiling around his stogie.

"You were worried about stepping on his toes too hard before."

The Democratic bigwig nodded. During Reconstruction, Democrats had called themselves "Conservatives" as if that were their party's name, ducking responsibility for their association with the Ku Klux, but since home rule was restored, they'd all gone back to being Democrats again.

"But if Hal does it right—which, I may add, he'd damn well better—it won't be us stepping on the bastard's toes. No badges, no official muscle. Leave it to the whitecaps or some other Yankee-hating crackers."

"And suppose they go too far?"

"I say again, we'll have no part in it and can't be held responsible for what the redneck riffraff does when they get liquored up and hear a Boston accent. Those hard feelings from the war die hard."

"Because I'm feeling out investors from the North," Dearborn explained. "Some of 'em have the Midas touch, seems like. If we can tap that motherlode it's like the Mississippi, good right on across the South."

"And good for *us*," said Arquette, smiling through a haze of blue tobacco smoke.

"That too."

"This fella may be rich and well received at home, but when the word gets out that he was down here chasing monsters, stirring up a hornet's nest by acting uppity, whatever happens to him won't rouse too much sympathy in Massachusetts or in Washington. He'll just be a crazy embarrassment to Yankee Land."

"I hope you're right, Grover," Dearborn replied.

"Relax, Noah. When have I ever let you down?"

"I want you to stay on him," Chief Hightower said.

"Just keep on watching 'im?" asked Yancy Osborn.

There were three of them this time, meeting behind dive called Beauregard's Retreat, although as far as Olson knew, no one named Beauregard had ever been associated with the place. Push come to shove, who even gave a damn?

"Just watching him until I tell you different," said Hightower. "But let me know if he spends time with anybody special."

"Counting Jubal Kenfield?"

"Anybody else," Hightower said.

"Just watching 'im," Yancy repeated, as if he could not believe it.

"If he gets too pushy, starts to throw his weight around, you may need to discourage him."

"How bad?" asked Yancy, smiling now.

"Depends on provocation, I suppose."

"Okay. I hear you."

"And if something happens to him—I mean something serious—there has to be a decent explanation."

"Like he picked a fight or something?"

"Maybe like that, or he could have an accident."

Olson nodded. "Sure. I've seen it happen lots a times."

"Nothing that could be traced back," Hightower stressed. "I wouldn't take it kindly otherwise."

Yancy knew well enough what *that* meant. Lethal accidents were not confined to nosy strangers from the North, by any means.

"Leave it to me," he told the chief.

"You got that backwards," Hightower advised him. "*You* leave it to *me*. Watch over him or have your people do it, someone you can trust. Report whatever you come up with, but don't move against him unless *I* say so. You understand me?"

"I ain't hard of hearing," Yancy said, beginning to get irritated now.

"I'll tell you when if and when to move, then leave the method up to you. Don't lift a finger until then."

"No problem, Chief."

"There'd better not be."

"If you don't trust me 'n the boys..."

"I didn't say that," Hightower cut Yancy off, retreating slightly from his tough guy act. "Just bear in mind the Powers That Be are looking down on both of us, and they don't listen to excuses if a job goes sideways."

Olson knew what that meant, but he still resented anybody casting doubt upon his competency.

"All right then," said the chief. "I'm headed home for supper but you need to get in touch with me, send someone by the house."

Hightower lived alone most of the time, but sometimes entertained Bess Goddard of a weekend, widowed long before her normal time of life. Yancy had crept around the chief's house, spying on them now and then, wondering why the lawman didn't close his bedroom curtains half the time.

Careless, maybe. Or else he thought his badge made him invincible around Natchez, so that he didn't have to care what anybody saw or thought about it.

And if that was true, it told Yancy the chief wasn't as smart as he might think he was.

"Talk to you later, then," said Hightower, moving off in the direction of his little house on Franklin Street.

Olson mounted his varnish Appaloosa, steered it toward the Haverstock Hilltop, and only spent about ten minutes killing time before his man appeared, riding his jet-black stallion from the alleyway that served the hotel's stable. Yancy gave him a head start, then trailed him at a safe distance, surprised to find Thorn heading for the colored part of town.

As far as Yancy knew, white men only had one of four reasons for a trip to Bronzeville. They were hoping to find cheap moonshine, brown sugar, cheap day labor, or some heathen hoodoo charm.

Maybe the man from Boston had another reason that eluded Olson, but it hardly mattered.

Visiting the wrong side of the tracks was dangerous enough for local whites who knew their way around.

For strangers it could be the kiss of death.

SIX

CEMETERY ROAD, NATCHEZ

Thorn didn't like the rural highway's name but understood it. Just a mile or so due north of town—the same direction that he'd traveled earlier, but inland from the river—he discovered Natchez City Cemetery, row on row of monuments and simpler headstones sprouting moss that masked some of the local names.

He knew this was the white folks' cemetery, while the town's ex-slaves maintained another of their own, in keeping with state segregation laws, or buried their departed loved ones close to home. Twelve years after the Civil War, it seemed to Thorn that nothing much had changed in Mississippi and, in fact, might never change if the white power structure had its way.

Congress had passed the Thirteenth Amendment's ban on slavery in January 1865, with twenty-seven states accepting it by year's end. Mississippi led the stubborn four refusing, joined by Delaware, Kentucky and New Jersey. The Garden State signed on in January 1866, but Mississippi and the other two—slave states that never left the Union when the South seceded—still stood fast, refusing to be swayed.

Not that it mattered, since the same amendment they declined to ratify still legally applied to them, at least in theory. Mississippi *had* ratified the Fourteenth and Fifteenth Amendments, granting former slaves full citizenship and voting rights, in January 1870, the price of readmission for their legislators into Congress, but from what Thorn had observed first-hand, those rules had no effect at all on blacks in the Magnolia State. As soon as armed whites had "redeemed" state government that same year, ex-slaves lost whatever ground they'd gained in Reconstruction, "free" on paper but the very opposite in fact.

With that background, Thorn hadn't been surprised to learn from Armond Joslin that still-unnamed contact from Adams County's black community would not meet Gideon at home, for safety's sake. And since no blacks aside from janitors could legally set foot inside the Haverstock Hilltop hotel, a rendezvous outside of town had been arranged with all the caution of a Union spy approaching closet Mississippi abolitionists during the war.

It had occurred to Thorn that clandestine meeting might turn out to be a trap. If Armond Joslin shared the views of other Mississippi white supremacists—which seemed entirely plausible—he might seek to intimidate or even murder Thorn by setting up an ambush in the countryside. Withdrawal of the Union's occupying troops from Dixie had, in fact, unleashed a tidal wave of racist violence that toppled "radical" state governments in three states where they still survived in early spring, just past.

The marker for Thorn's meeting with his secretive informant was a giant oak tree, gnarled with age and blackened on its north side by a lightning strike years earlier. Approaching it, he sent Shadow a soothing message and unhooked the hammer thongs that held his twin Colt Peacemakers securely in their holsters.

Anything might happen now, and Gideon had taken all precautions that he could, short of refusing to appear. Jubal Kenfield was at his office, working on tomorrow's issue of the *Natchez Independent,* waiting to hear back from Thorn or sound alarms if Gideon did not return.

That wouldn't help, of course, if he was lying dead on Cemetery Road, but when Obi Magoro and Thorn's lawyers got in touch, at least Kenfield could outline Thorn's last movements and name Armond Joslin as the likely architect of his demise.

Not that white law would move against a Mississippian of Joslin's wealth and stature.

But a vengeance-minded African just might.

Down range, a black man stepped out from behind the great oak, hands out to his sides with fingers splayed, to indicate he was unarmed. Thorn urged his stallion slowly forward, sharp eyes flicking left and right in search of any lurking ambushers and finding none.

When he was near enough to speak without raising his voice, Thorn introduced himself and waited for the stranger to reply.

"Erasmus Finch," his one-man welcoming committee said. "I got word from a friend that you look into things that most men won't and solve some problems that they can't."

"I make no promises," Gideon said, "beyond my own best effort and a fair hearing of anything you want to share. I've been of help sometimes, but others not so much."

"No man can do more than his best," Finch answered. "And around here, most white men don't even try."

Thorn nodded. Said, "It's been an education, stopping here."

"You hunt the thing that's killing people on the river?"

"First, I need to find out whether it exists."

"Oh, it exists, all right. You want to talk about it more, we need to find us a more private spot."

"Lead on," Thorn said.

"Just get my transportation, then," Finch said, and stepped behind the oak. Thorn gripped the curved butt of his right-hand Colt, then let it go when Finch returned, trailing a donkey on a lead.

"I never got them forty acres," he said, smiling. "But this here's my mule."

Yancy Olson was doubly cautious this time, following the man in black out Cemetery Road. He stayed well back and out of sight, glad now that he'd turned out alone instead of trying to enlist another whitecap as backup.

He didn't have a clue where Thorn was headed, out here in the country north of town, but saw his quarry slowing on approach to a great oak well known to every local resident. Steering his varnish Appaloosa off the road, ducking behind a stand of smaller trees, he cautiously dismounted, going down on all fours as he crept back to the road's edge, watching Thorn rein in.

Yancy was watching as a black man stepped out from behind the oak with his hands raised. The sound of voices talking back and forth reached Olson's ears, but he was too far back to make out any words. The field hand's face *did* look familiar, never mind Yancy's belief that all black men looked pretty much the same.

Searching his brain to match a name up with that face,

however, Yancy drew a blank. It nagged at him and still might surface later, but for now, he tried to memorize specifics of the black man's looks for future reference.

In case his master's voice commanded him to track the darky down and have a word with him in private—or erase him from existence, as the case might be.

After a couple minutes gabbing, Olson saw the black man duck behind the oak again and come back with a mule. He mounted up and rode off northward, side by side with Thorn. If Yancy had been sensitive to irony—or if he even knew the word at all—it might have struck him oddly that a white New Englander, dressed up from head to toe in black, had traveled fifteen hundred miles southward from home to meet a black man by the side of Cemetery Road.

But as it was, all Yancy understood was that he had a job to do, trailing the Yankee and whoever he met up with, find out what they were discussing, and report back to Chief Hightower with all dispatch.

His problem now was that he still had nothing to report.

Before he met the chief again, Olson would either have to dredge the black man's name up from his memory or maybe trail Thorn with his guide back to the darky's residence and mark it down for future action. Barring either breakthrough he would only make the chief mad as a hornet, and that would rebound on Yancy to his detriment.

Whoever served the Natchez power structure well derived a measure of respect and privilege for helping realize the Democratic Party's goal of white supremacy eternal. On the other hand, a man who tried and failed was worse than useless. Knowledge he'd accumulated could be turned to evidence of criminality in court, which meant that failures to the cause weren't simply cast aside.

They were eliminated to ensure their silence everlasting.

"That ain't me," Olson advised his Appaloosa in a near stage whisper. "That ain't me at all, and if I go, I'm taking others down with me."

COTTONWOOD ROAD

"This'll be the first time that I ever had a white man over to my house," Erasmus Finch told Thorn. "Whitecaps uninvited, come by eight or nine months, but my wife and I were elsewhere at the time."

"Forewarned," Gideon guessed.

"We mostly stick together here in Bronzeville," Finch replied. "Or them that don't, decide it ain't a healthy place to stick around."

The house they were approaching was another shotgun model, but it hadn't gone to seed after the fashion of the shack where Purnell Thomas lived. Thorn was surprised a vigilante mob had left it standing and said so.

"I can't rightly account for that," Finch said. "They busted out a couple windows and one of 'em did his business on the porch, but you could say we got off easy. Maybe they weren't drunk enough to go all out, or maybe they had other calls to make that night."

"No trouble since then?" Thorn inquired.

"I took my name off of the county voting register," Finch said, sounding embarrassed to admit as much. "That only left four freedmen listed, and they're all gone now. Three pulled up stakes. The fourth one died in a house fire. Coroner claims that lightning hit his place."

"You doubt it?"

"I was fishing on the river that night. Not a cloud for miles around, nor any sound of thunder."

"If you'd rather not discuss this at your home..."

"My wife—that's Caddie—went to visit neighbors, so it's only you and me. Somebody else shows up, I'll handle it."

Dismounting from Shadow, he walked the stallion out of sight from passersby and left it grazing in the woods out back as sunset hurried on. Inside, the house was spotless, with the fragrance of a recent homecooked meal, a polar opposite from the malodorous squalor of Purnell Travis's abode.

"I got some coffee from this afternoon that should be palatable," Finch said, "or a taste of shine if you'd like something stronger."

"Coffee's good," Thorn said, and thanked his host as he received a steaming mug.

When Finch was settled at the kitchen table with a glass of homemade liquor set in front of him, Gideon said, "I understand from Armond Joslin that this creature, whatever it is, showed up again last night, across the river on Louisiana's side."

"Could be."

"Could be, or is?" Thorn pressed.

Finch sipped and said, "It's family and I don't like to drag them into this."

"No reason they should ever see or hear from me," Thorn said.

"You need to keep in mind I ain't seen nothing of this critter for myself. Word gets around and all."

"I understand. About last night..."

"Two men went out for catfish, late on in the evening. They never made it back, but people found their skiff capsized and nosed against the bank a half mile down from Ferriday."

"Physical damage?"

"Not enough to sink it, but there's talk about scratch marks and gouges on the hull, for whatever that's worth."

"Maybe a drifting log?"

"It's possible. Not likely, though."

"Why not?"

"One of 'em was a cousin on my mama's side, named Lucius Reeves. The other was a friend of his called Alvy Lauber."

"Could they swim?"

"Like walleyes," Finch replied. "Both of 'em grew up on the river and been fishing it since they were knee-high to a badger. That don't mean they *couldn't* drown, mind you, but losing two of them together? I can't picture that."

"So, you think they were taken?"

"Saying that they *could have* been. Don't know for sure, but night's supposed to be when this thing comes around most often. Night's when Lucius liked to go out fishing with Alvy."

"Why then?" asked Thorn.

"Keeping their health in mind."

"It sounds more dangerous than during daytime."

"Did I mention Alvy Lauber was a white man?"

"No, you didn't."

"Well, it makes a difference in Mississippi, maybe more than any other place below the Mason-Dixon Line. White men are bosses, even if they fall out on the poor side. Whites tell coloreds what to do and when. Palling around together ain't just frowned upon, you know. In Mississippi it's a criminal offense."

"Ridiculous and shameful," Thorn said.

"But it's still the law. No reason to believe I'll ever see it changed."

Thorn knew he couldn't change a whole state's mind or mores, so he sipped his coffee and replied, "I take it that you think this creature's real."

"I think there's *something* out there on the prowl but couldn't tell you what it is or where it comes from."

"And I suspect that you've been thinking over what to do about it."

"Might have done," Finch granted.

"Anything you want to share?" asked Gideon.

Erasmus answered with a question of his own.

"What do you know about submersibles?"

THE NATCHEZ INDEPENDENT'S OFFICE

Jubal Kenfield had finished setting type for Friday's issue and had run a proof copy. Now he was reading over it, scanning for errors that he could correct before he let the offset press begin to clank and clatter.

He was halfway through the front page—one of eight all told—when he was suddenly distracted by the bell over the street door to his office. "Be right out!" he called from the backroom, then used a pencil stub to mark where he'd stopped reading and went out to greet the new arrival.

What he saw in the reception area brought him up short, unable to conceal his obvious surprise.

"Mr. Dearborn. How are you, sir?"

"Jubal," the banker replied, "haven't I asked you time and time again to call me Noah?"

"Yes, sir. I can't seem to get the hang of it, if you'll forgive me. With a man in your position..."

Kenfield couldn't think of any more to say and left the sentence fragment handing there between them.

"I get that sometimes," Dearborn granted. "But I'm really just a man."

And Midas, Jubal thought, *was just a king from Greek mythology touch turned anything he handled into solid gold. Too bad the greedy bastard starved to death because he couldn't feed himself.*

"I'll try hard to remember that, Noah."

"In fact, that's why I'm here," said Dearborn. "I've got business to discuss with you."

"Well, that's good news," Jubal enthused. "I could stop by at your convenience in the morning, once I've put the morning paper out."

Dearborn allowed himself a small frown. "It's tomorrow's issue that I need to speak with you about, Jubal."

Kenfield's stomach clenched up, as if he were preparing to receive a punch. He swallowed with some difficulty. Said, "I always welcome the opinions and suggestions of my readers."

"Excellent. That's what I hoped you'd say."

"And this is in regard to...what, again?"

"Your recent visitor from Yankee Land," Dearborn replied.

"Ah. Mr. Thorn."

"The very same."

"You've met him, then?" Kenfield inquired.

"I haven't had the pleasure, Jubal."

Though he never would have thought it possible, Kenfield was swiftly tiring of the banker saying his first name.

"You might enjoy his company," the newsman

ventured. "If you like, I could arrange an introduction for the two of you and—"

"No."

After a rapid eye blink, Kenfield asked, "Then what's this all about?"

"I hear you've gotten chummy with the man," Dearborn replied. "Perhaps a bit too close, in fact."

"I've interviewed him for a feature story on his visit," Kenfield said.

"And then went drinking with him at The Brass Rail, I believe it was."

"Am I under surveillance, Noah?"

"Lord, no! Jubal, you rank high among Natchez celebrities, by virtue of your trade and public voice. Most people in the in the city share respect for you."

Most, Jubal absorbed, keeping his mouth shut for the moment.

Noah Dearborn filled the silence that spun out between them. "It would be a shame for that to change, don't you agree?"

"Why should it?"

"Well...you understand that Natchez is a growing city. Some aspects are still recuperating from the war."

"That's true across the South, Noah."

"Exactly! And in times of active competition, it's imperative for all Natchezians to put their best foot forward. Put the city's best *face* forward, eh?"

"I'm still not sure I follow you," Kenfield replied. In fact, he had begun to follow Dearborn very well indeed, and didn't like where this was headed.

"Take this 'monster' foolishness, for instance. If a paper like the *Independent* touts that as legitimate, it could derail outstanding plans to bring new industry and capital investment into Adams County."

"I'm not planning any features on this creature at the moment," Kenfield said.

"But you're reporting on a handsome Yankee coming in to hunt it, making those who question its existence look like fools and country bumpkins."

"Not at all," said Jubal, bristling now. "You ought to read an article before you criticize its contents, Noah."

"Listen, will you, Jubal? I have nothing against Mr. Thorn or his peculiar theories. If he wants to chase a dragon or whatever, simply let him chase it somewhere else. In Texas, say, where they claim everything grows bigger."

"He's already done that, as you'll find out when you read the piece."

"Jubal, why are you making this so difficult?"

"What am I making difficult?"

"A friendly resolution of this matter."

"I see nothing to resolve, Mr. Dearborn. If, when you've read the article, you have some criticism of it, I'd be pleased to print your letter saying so."

"But will the *Independent* still be here a week from Friday, Jubal?"

"State your business," Kenfield answered. "Say it plain."

"All right, then. If you run this monster-hunting feature in the morning, I suspect you'll feel a strong adverse reaction from your advertisers. Maybe you can churn out papers for another month or so with no income, if you've laid by a stockpile of supplies. Beyond that...well, I have my doubts."

"Message received," said Jubal. "Now, if you'll excuse me, I'm a busy man and so are you."

"Indeed," said Dearborn, turning toward the street

door. "It appears that I have many other stops to make this evening."

It smelled like Chief Hightower must be frying pork when Yancy Olson rapped on his backdoor. The chief appeared a moment later, but left Olson standing where he was, no WELCOME mat under his feet, instead of asking him inside.

"Sorry for interrupting supper," Yancy said.

The chief ignored that, looking down at him and asking, "Are you done with Thorn?"

"Not quite," Olson replied.

"The hell's that mean, 'not quite'?"

"I followed 'im out Cemetery Road until he met a nigger at the big old oak out there."

"And?"

"So, they talked a while. I couldn't get in close enough to hear 'em, else they would've spotted me."

"And you just left 'em out there?"

"No, sir. First off, I thought I recognized the nigger, but I couldn't place 'im till he took the Yankee back to his place."

"And?" the chief repeated.

"And I *do* know 'im. Erasmus Finch, one a them shines what put 'is name down on the voter rolls last year."

"And took it off again when he got wise," Hightower said.

"After some a my whitecaps paid a visit to 'im."

"When he wasn't home, as I recall."

Worried that he was blushing, Olson toed the dirt and muttered, "Anyway, he got the message, right?"

"But now he's hosting Thorn at home. And what do you suppose that's all about?"

"Told you I couldn't overhear 'em, Chief. But Thorn's here looking for that river monster, right? He must think Finch knows something that'll help him."

"As it happens, he just might," Hightower said. "He might have heard something from Chief Mayberry, over there in Vidalia. A couple fishermen went out last night, cat trolling, and they ain't come home yet. Skiff washed up with damage, and it looks like something tipped 'em over."

"So?"

"So, Chief Mayberry asks me do I know one of the lost men has a cousin over here in Natchez. Wanna guess who that is?"

"Finch?"

"Got it in one."

"Goddamn it! What about the other guy?"

"A white man, if you can believe it. No connection over this side that they know of yet."

"Race-mixing!" Olson spat the words out like a curse.

"And now we got the cousin over here, consorting with another white man, and a Boston Yankee, too."

"It's all connected, Chief. It's gotta be!"

"Sounds like something the whitecaps should investigate, don't you think?"

"You're goddamn right I do!"

"See to it, then," Hightower said. And closed the door in Olson's face.

SEVEN

COTTONWOOD ROAD

"You mean the underwater boats some people have called submarines?"

Erasmus Finch nodded. "The very same," he said.

In fact, Thorn knew what northern journalists had published following the Civil War, when censorship was standard policy, when he was still an undergraduate at Boston's Weatherford Academy. Sometime during the reign of Charles V, king of Spain and Holy Roman Emperor, during the 1550s, two Greeks had performed a demonstration with an underwater boat they had devised, emerging with their clothes dry and a candle they had covered still burning. In 1578, English mathematician William Bourne had published plans for a submersible but never got around to building it. Eighteen years later, Scottish scientist and theologian John Napier wrote of plans for underwater "sailing" craft to strike at hostile warships. In 1620 Dutchman Cornelis Drebbel built a submarine powered by oars for

King James I of England. During the 1740s British courts granted at least a dozen patents for proposed submersibles.

American David Bushnell produced the first military submarine, christened *Turtle*, in 1775, with room aboard for a single operator who powered its screws with a hand crank. Another American, Robert Fulton of steam engine fame, designed the *Nautilus* for France in 1800, but Emperor Napoleon Bonaparte canceled the project four years later.

Next came the Civil War, when both sides constructed submersibles for use in combat. The Confederacy fared better than its northern rivals, starting with the CSS *Pioneer*. Yankee forces captured that submarine, but Dixie rebounded with the CSS *David* and CSS *H. L. Hunley*, producing mixed results. Between October 1863 and March 1864, they attacked several Union warships, sinking the USS *Housatonic* in Charleston harbor with a "spar torpedo"—a wooden pole tipped with explosives for ramming. Abe Lincoln's navy sank the *Housatonic* hours after that attack, and Union soldiers captured several submarines at Charleston in February 1865.

Sailing on freedom's side, the Union commissioned the twelve-man, 275-ton USS *Alligator*, armed with detachable magnetic mines, but the bulky craft never saw combat. Meanwhile, France launched the *Plongeur*—"Diver"—in 1863 and Spain produced the *Ictineo II* a year later. Since Appomattox, Julius Kröhl had built the *Sub Marine Explorer* for America and Chile had used the *Flach* to protect the port of Valparaiso from Spanish warships during the Chincha Islands War. That same year, British engineer Robert Whitehead had pioneered a "locomotive torpedo" fired underwater, to replace the older spar ramming model.

"Why mention that?" Thorn asked his host.

Finch hesitated for a moment, then cracked a smile. "Because I've got one," he replied.

"A submarine?"

"One of the Rebel boats," Finch said. "It's not a big one, only seats three men, but with the right equipment I reckon it just might finish off whatever's plaguing folks all up and down the river."

Thorn saw a certain logic to it, but he focused on the drawbacks first.

"Two problems I can think of," he told Finch. "We'd need to work out what the creature is, and then we'd have to find it."

Nodding, Finch said, "I already thought of that. But are we in agreement that there *is* something to hunt?"

"I spoke to Purnell Travis earlier today," said Thorn.

"The first mate from the *Faust*."

"That's him. He's on the bottle now but something obviously terrified him at the time. He's still saying that some monstrous thing he's never seen before attacked his boat."

"And ate the crew," Finch added.

"As to that," Thorn said, "he isn't claiming that he witnessed anything. I didn't get the feeling he was dressing up his story for attention. If he made up the whole thing, it's backfired on him. He's convinced that everyone in Natchez hates him now or thinks he's lost his mind."

"And what do you think, having met 'im?" Finch asked.

"I believe he saw *something* but can't say what it was. I also took a ride to see the *Faust* this morning, or what's left of it. There's no denying that its keel struck something large enough to make it capsize."

"I was born near here and I've been living on the Mississippi ever since," Finch said. "There's gators in the river, sure enough. They'll eat you, given half a chance. I've seen some whoppers for myself, too close for comfort, but the biggest one I ever saw was thirteen, maybe fourteen feet from nose on back. You'd need the great granddaddy of 'em all to shake a paddle wheeler, much less flip it over."

"I agree," Thorn said. "But I've seen bigger things and science recognizes some of them."

He didn't mention Texas or its flying dragon, knowing that was hard to grasp for anyone who had not seen it in the scaly flesh.

"You're talkin about what they call a dinosaur," Finch said.

"Well..."

"What I understand, they all died out a long, long time ago. People are digging up their bones these days, putting 'em back together in museums."

Thorn eschewed behaving like a know-it-all but took a chance. "I studied them a bit in school, back east. Newspapers toss all the giant prehistoric lizards into one bag, but the scientists that research only treat creatures that lived on land as proper dinosaurs. The ones with wings, flying around, are labeled pterosaurs, meaning 'winged lizards.' In the ancient lakes and oceans there were swimming air-breathers, at least ten taxonomic genera."

"What's that mean?" Finch inquired.

"Biologists draw charts to classify all life on Earth. Genera rank between the family and species. It's a way of sorting plants and animals to make sense out of evolution."

"Like Charles Darwin wrote before the war, that book that got the preachers all riled up."

"Exactly right," said Thorn. "*The Origin of Species.* If you plan to hunt an animal, it helps to know where it belongs in nature, size and diet, all of that."

"And whether it could still be living in the world today."

"Something we ought to figure out," Thorn said, "before we start off tracking it."

"Is everybody clear on what we gotta do?" asked Yancy Olson.

Ranged before him, half a dozen of his trusted white-caps nodded, some adding muttered assent. One of them, Dwight Peckham, spoke up, saying, "Get the niggers!"

Yancy swallowed back a sigh, replying, "This is more about the Yankee. Do you all get that? We ran the carpet-baggers off already, and it's time to show 'em that it ain't worth coming back for seconds."

"Do we kill 'im right off?" asked Jesse Reese.

"The main thing's that he high-tails outa Natchez and keeps going till he's someone else's aggravation. But for damn sure, if pulls on you, do whatever you gotta do about it."

"Plenty places we can dump him in the Homochitto," Gavin Grisby volunteered. "Gators will scarf him down and won't leave nothin' for the law to find."

He was referring to the Homochitto swamp and forest, more than 190,000 acres of wilderness stretching from Natchez to Brookhaven, spanning much of Adams, Franklin and Lincoln Counties—the latter ironically named for late President Abe. Yancy could only guess how many blacks and Radical Republicans had found their final resting places in that wilderness, although he'd helped with planting some of them himself.

"I'm keeping that in mind," he told Grisby. "But what

you-all need to remember is we're doing this for Natchez and the good of every pure white soul in Adams County. If this guy from Boston has his way, our town will be a laughingstock or worse, someplace where monsters run around snacking on anybody they can catch."

"More nigger superstition," Elwood Vinton growled.

"We do this right," Yancy reminded him, "we'll have the gratitude of everyone who matters hereabouts. We screw it up, and that could go another way entirely. Are you with me?"

All six voices answered with a rebel yell.

"All right, then. Mount up and let's get a move one while we still got time."

THE NATCHEZ INDEPENDENT OFFICE

Jubal Kenfield had not felt this nervous since he'd first set foot in Natchez.

Noah Dearborn's visit, with his clear threat of an economic boycott and a hint of worse to come, had made up Jubal's mind that he'd be sleeping at the *Independent's* office overnight and standing guard over the printing press that was equivalent to his survival. While the oiled machinery was clanking, spitting out pages of newsprint that he'd have to collate and fold himself before distributing tomorrow's issue, Kenfield made adjustments to the pistol tucked under his belt, around in back and out of sight but primed to fire at need.

He'd never fired a shot at any living thing before tonight —much less trying to wound or kill a man—but any yokel stricken with an urge to wreck his office or prevent front-page story circulating would be in for a surprise.

His piece was a .28-caliber Colt Model 1855 Sidehammer pocket revolver, loaded with five rounds in its cylinder. It weighed seventeen ounces, tugging down his slacks a bit in back, and measured nine inches overall with its 4.5-inch octagonal barrel. The manufacturer cited the weapon's effective range as twenty-five yards, roughly three times the distance from his backroom to the street outside.

Whether he could hit anything at that distance remained a mystery, but at the very least, Kenfield was ready to produce a hellish racket and a haze of smoke before a prowler could retaliate.

And if he died defending his interpretation of the Constitution's First Amendment...well, he'd hardly be the first.

Before he started printing out tomorrow morning's paper, Kenfield had fortified himself with two stiff shots of sour mash whiskey. Some drinkers called that whiskey bourbon, but as Jubal understood his booze, the latter tag only applied to liquor distilled in Kentucky. By whatever name, the alcohol had raised his flagging spirits, giving him a sense—likely misplaced—that he could fend off anyone who tried to censor him.

As for the advertisers who might well desert him prior to next week's issue, there was nothing he could do about that now.

If one self-styled dictator in a three-piece suit could tell the *Independent* which stories to print, which to ignore, Kenfield decided that he might as well pack up and leave Natchez, maybe the whole damned state, and possibly the South itself.

Or he could fight, if it came down to that.

And if that happened, Jubal was determined that he would not go alone.

COTTONWOOD ROAD

"When can I have a look at that submersible?" Thorn asked.

"It's hidden," Finch replied. "Not far away, but there's no point in going off to see it after dark. Weather like this, rattlers and copperheads are hunting in the woods, and cottonmouths if you stray too close to the water. Anytime tomorrow should be fine."

They'd come to no conclusion on what kind of creature might be wreaking havoc on the Mississippi. Thorn agreed with Finch that no mere alligator could have wrecked the *Faust*, and he believed the same was true of the larger American crocodile.

As for a giant relict from the distant past surviving into modern times, Gideon couldn't rule it out but had no book of illustrations handy that depicted their presumed appearance from excavated, reassembled bones. Besides, which, even if he'd had a book like that on hand, their only living witness—Purnell Travis—couldn't swear to what he'd briefly glimpsed in darkness, much less narrow down the list of suspects to a single prehistoric species.

As it stood, they had a vehicle or weapon to employ, assuming that the Rebel submarine was still in any shape to sail, but no idea of where or how to find their prey.

"Shall I come back then, in the morning? If you'd rather meet me somewhere else..."

"Nope. Here is fine, as long as—"

Finch stopped dead in mid-sentence, eyes narrowing as he looked past Thorn, through his home's front window facing the road. Gideon turned, followed his gaze, and spotted seven riders, all disguised by hoods and robes as if portraying ghosts for Halloween—or All Saints Eve, as some preferred. Each rider hat at least one pistol strapped around his waist and four of them were bearing torches.

"Goddamn whitecaps," Finch advised. "Been hoping that I'd seen the last of 'em."

"This could be my fault," Thorn replied. "I saw nobody following me out from town, but it's a possibility. If someone knows the roads and landscape well enough, I could have missed them."

"Too late now to fret about it," Finch said. "Best if you go out the back and get away from here quick as you can."

Go out the back, Thorn mused. Where Shadow waited, doubtless with his ears perked, following the new arrivals.

Waiting with Thorn's Winchester secured in his saddle boot.

"We know you're in there, Rastus!" Yancy Olson shouted through his hood made from a flour sack. "You'd best get out here double-quick, before we have to come inside and fetch you!"

Yancy didn't care much for his homemade mask. It couldn't hold a candle to the headpiece that he'd once worn as a member of the Adams County Ku Klux Klan, complete with devil's horns, a big hooked nose, and trailing whiskers made from Spanish moss. White vigilantes had a certain style back then, during the wicked Reconstruction days, but now had fallen on hard times.

No matter, though. He still got just as big a thrill from night-riding as ever, bullying the freedmen and their wives, keeping the darkies in their place as carefully ordained by Mississippi's white society.

Ten second passed, then Yancy tried again. "This is your last chance, Rastus! Get your ass out here before we torch the place with you and your damned Yankee in it."

Now the front door opened, and a dark face Olson recognized regarded them with an expression Yancy couldn't place, torchlight reflected on their target's prominent cheekbones.

"My name's Erasmus," Finch advised, "not Rastus. Maybe you're mixed up on where you mean to be?"

"We got the right place, nigger," Olson sneered at him —kind of a waste, what with his face concealed. "Step outa the house and let us see your hands."

"I's comin', Boss," Finch said, his mocking tone the next thing to backhand slap. And as he cleared the shack's front door, he held a double-barreled shotgun braced against his hip.

The sound of pistols cocking on both sides of Olson sounded like twigs snapping under clumsy feet. The shotgun's twin muzzles, aimed at Yancy's chest, seemed large enough to suck him in and spit him out again.

"You know what's good for you, you'll drop that scattergun right now, boy," Yancy said.

" 'Fraid I can't do that, Boss," Finch said, no doubt about his mocking tone this time. "I's scared it might go off and kill somebody accidental like."

Deciding that a change of subject might defuse the situation long enough for one or more whitecaps to put Finch down, Finch answered, "You were told to bring that visitor o' yours outside. Where is he?"

"He's right here," said a voice from Olson's right.

Yancy turned toward the sound and saw the Yankee dressed in black, as for a funeral, sighting along the barrel of his shouldered Winchester.

. . .

Finch heard Thorn's voice but didn't shift his eyes in that direction. If he dropped his guard for even a split-second, it could get him killed.

He thanked God that his wife wasn't at home when the whitecaps arrived. She wouldn't have to witness whatever was coming next, or risk her life trying to join the fight that seemed inevitable now.

The whitecap leader cautioned Thorn, "You don't know what you're doing, boy. Have you got any notion who we are?"

Thorn answered with a question of his own. "A bunch of peckerwoods afraid to show their faces?"

"Goddamn you, Mister! We don't want your kind around Natchez."

"And just when I was starting to feel right at home," Thorn said.

"That smart mouth's just about to get you killed," the leader said.

In other circumstance, Finch might well have laughed, seeing the way his homespun mask puffed out with each word spoken, dropping back between them.

"Is harsh language all you've got?" Thorn challenged the nightriders. "If it is, you may as well turn tail."

"To hell with this!" one of the other whitecaps snarled, yanking a six-gun from his cross-draw holster, swinging it toward Thorn.

Before the masked man had a chance to fire, a rifle shot cracked out, a slug punched through the gunman's shoulder, and he toppled from his saddle with a squeal of pain. His pistol fired its load off toward the pale three-quarters moon above.

As other whitecaps drew their sidearms, Finch squeezed off one barrel of his scattergun, angling its buckshot toward a swath of air a foot or so above their shrouded heads. One pellet grazed a rider's scalp regardless, wringing out a bleat of pain and fear before he swung his horse around and spurred it back toward Natchez.

After that, it didn't take long, mopping up. None of the whitecaps chose to stay and fight, the limit of their courage voiced in shouted curses as they wheeled away, intent on getting out of range. The man who Thorn had toppled from his horse managed to rise and lurch after his friends on foot, howling, "Don't shoot no more, damn you!"

Thorn fired another rifle shot, raising a puff of dust beside the runner's feet, and sped him on his way.

"Well, damn!" Finch muttered to himself. "That tears it now."

Thorn came around the corner, saw Finch standing on his doorstep, shotgun smoking in his hands.

"Could have been worse," he offered, knowing that it sounded feeble.

"Not for me," Finch said. "Soon as those fools get back to town, Chief Hightower will likely deputize them and their kin to come back here and burn me out."

"It feels like my fault," Gideon replied. "If you need money for the road, to get away..."

"Ain't necessary," Finch said. "What I meant is that I can't stay *here,* this place. I need to get my wife clear, then we've got a monster waiting for us on the river."

"If your safety is at risk—"

"That's nothing new," Finch said. "Show me a colored man who ain't at risk in Mississippi, and you've found yourself a boot-licker. I told you I was born and raised in Adams County. Only way I'm leaving it is when the good Lord fixes my reward or punishment on Judgment Day."

Thorn faced him squarely. Said, "You pulled your shot."

"You did the same," Finch countered. "That is, 'less you normally miss targets like that fat boy, only winging 'im."

"I didn't think it served our purposes by killing them," said Thorn. "Yours least of all."

"So, we've got seven whitecaps running back to town, one of 'em wounded, with the other six getting their stories straight for the police. You don't think they'll be coming after you, as well as me?"

Thorn frowned and answered Finch's question with another. "How late does your Western Union office operate?"

Finch blinked at him, confused. Finally said, "They've got somebody there around the clock, if you can trust 'em."

"I'll make sure they send the message straight."

"Calling for help?"

"Waking my lawyers up in Boston. They get cranky after hours and they'll pass that on to their connections at the capital, in Jackson."

"They got any pull with our state's governor? 'Cause, if they don't—"

Thorn interrupted him, saying, "They've got a line on anybody nationwide who wants to see his state do well from industry and capital investments. You're the one we need to think about, you and your wife."

In fact, Thorn wasn't altogether sure of that, but if worse came to worst, he still had ample firepower.

"All right, if you say so. I'm getting out of here before them whitecaps drink enough Dutch courage to come back and try their luck again."

"Where can we meet to talk some more about that submarine?" Thorn asked.

"You're at the Hilltop?"

"Right."

"I'll send word in the morning, through a friend of mine. Don't be surprised when you see that he's white."

EIGHT

THE HAVERSTOCK HILLTOP HOTEL: JUNE 22, 1877

Thorn had slept with guns around him through the night, expecting trouble any moment. Dozing off wasn't a problem for him, though, as he had been in tight spots previously, where his life and others that he cared about were riding on the line.

His first stop, back in Natchez, had been at the Western Union office, rousting out a drowsy clerk and dictating a message to the Boston law firm of Messrs. Block, Enright & Sloan, fire-breathing advocates who owed their fortunes chiefly to the Thorn estate. Gideon had not exaggerated when he told Erasmus Finch that his attorneys knew important people in all thirty-eight states and most of the ten territories still awaiting statehood. Gideon could not have said exactly *who* the firm could influence on his behalf in Mississippi, but he knew they always liked to start out at the top and then work down from there.

He had already shaved, dressed, and was buckling on

his pistols when the sound of rapping on his door distracted him. The knocking sounded angry, but Thorn didn't let that hurry him.

Police Chief Hightower was stood waiting in the hallway, cheeks mottled with a range of colors from maroon to cherry red. "We need to talk," he said, but made no effort to invade Thorn's rented room.

Stepping aside, Gideon said, "Come in. I've got a bit of time before breakfast."

When he had closed the door, Hightower rounded on him, glaring. Asked him, "What in Hell do you mean, bothering the governor?"

That, Thorn knew, would be John Marshall Stone, appointed to replace Adelbert Ames when that Republican stepped down in 1876, predicted to win in his own right this coming November.

"I've never met or spoken to the man," he told Hightower honestly.

"Well, through your layers, then. Why did I get a telegram direct from him last night, saying I'd better mind my p's and q's where you're concerned?"

"Chief," Thorn replied, "that question sounds like one I should be asking you."

"Goddamn it! What is *that* supposed to mean?"

"You want to play the fool, it's fine with me," Thorn said, his right hand resting on the curved butt of a Peacemaker. "Last night, a bunch of yahoos dressed like ghosts tried to attack me and a friend of mine. They had some bad luck, and I figured you or someone like you would come calling, trying to make out like he and I bear the responsibility for local felons tearing up the countryside."

"You and a *friend*, is it? When you ain't been a full day in Natchez? Would this friend be a nigger, Mr. Thorn?"

"And if he is a colored man, what of it?" Thorn replied. "Are you, the top lawman in town, about to say your laws only protect white citizens, and all the rest are fair game for whichever redneck pinhead comes along?"

Hightower looked as if he might suffer a stroke at any moment, but he brought his voice under control. "You ain't in Boston now," he said. "In Mississippi, we do things a little different than up in Massachusetts."

"Clearly, if you sanction hooded mobs running amok," Thorn said. "I hope you're smart enough to see how that might lead to repercussions for yourself and Natchez overall."

"And all that gibberish means, *what*, exactly?"

Thorn allowed himself a sigh before he said, "All right. It seems I was mistaken, so I'll spell it out for you. My lawyers rank among the best in these United States, of which your sainted Mississippi is a part. You may not like it, and you're not alone in that, by any means. But know this: Block, Enright and Sloan have influence with anyone who matters nationwide, including Washington, D.C. I understand your people made a deal with our new president to get the blue-coats out of Dixie, but I promise you, if can't do your job and keep the peace, they could be back again in nothing flat."

"You're bluffing," said Hightower, but his tone had lost some of its fire.

"So, call my bluff, Chief. Lock me up and tell your whitecap friends a time when they can try to lynch me. Send them off to hurt my friends in Natchez, where you've sworn an oath to maintain law and order. See how you're slapped with charges of conspiracy under the Ku Klux Act. When you're convicted, don't expect an easy ride in your own jail. I hear the U.S. courts prefer sending your kind off to the Dry Tortugas."

"I don't understand a goddamn thing you're saying!"

"I doubt that's true," Thorn said, "although I can't entirely rule it out. Try this, then. Tell your bedsheet buddy that the next time they come after me, they can expect their silly robes to serve as shrouds."

"That mouth of yours is gonna get you into trouble one day soon," Hightower said.

"It wouldn't be the first time, Chief."

"I ain't responsible for what comes next."

"And yet, I'm holding you responsible. So is your governor, and likely the U.S. Attorney General. Now, if you're finished making threats, we'll have to wrap this up. I'm late for breakfast."

Hightower produce a throat growl, then stormed out of Thorn's room. Gideon waited long enough for him to clear the hotel's lobby, then locked up and started on his way downstairs.

Thorn checked on Belle and Shadow in the hotel's stable, then walked down to Pepper Jack's, watching for any followers along the way. He spotted none and reached the restaurant in time to get another table by the window facing onto Silver Street.

The same blonde waitress from his visit yesterday was working, but she had more difficulty smiling at him this time. Gideon supposed it had to do with word of last night's shooting, which had doubtless made the rounds by now. Most of the other breakfast diners were pretending that they hadn't seen him enter, as if making eye contact would shift their names from loyal Mississippians to place them on the whitecaps' target list.

So be it.

It wasn't Thorn's first time confronting closed minds in a town that valued preservation of the status quo above hard facts and simple justice. He had seen the same tired drama acted out before, in Texas, and more recently in Arkansas. On both occasions it had nearly cost his life, but he had stuck it out, succeeded in his quests, and planned on doing so again.

Unless some cracker killed him first, that is.

Thorn ordered scrambled eggs with bacon, pancakes on the side, and coffee black. The waitress bobbed her head and scurried off to place his order with the chef, while Gideon observed the street, continuing his search for enemies who might not have learned a lesson from last night.

Instead, he spotted Jubal Kenfield, ducking in and out of shops with copies of the morning's *Natchez Independent*. When the publisher crossed over Silver Street and entered Pepper Jack's, he left some papers on the counter, then retreated, greeting customers he recognized along the way.

Before he reached the exit, Kenfield saw Thorn watching him and veered off-course to take a seat at Gideon's table for two. Hunched forward, almost whispering, he said, "I heard about the ruckus last night. Was that you, by any chance?"

Thorn smiled and said, "It's news to me."

"All right, then. But be careful who you're dealing with from now on. I'm already taking heat about this morning's profile on you, when nobody else had any chance to read it before now."

"If that's a problem for you—"

"Not at all," the newsman said, not quite convincingly. "I need to get a move on now, but don't let down your guard."

"I never do," Thorn said, and watched Jubal retreat just as his morning meal arrived.

THE LOWER MISSISSIPPI RIVER

The predator swims silently along, sharp eyes scanning the dark water ahead of it and off to either side. It swims against the current, northbound, after drifting with the river's flow last night, past Baton Rouge and halfway to New Orleans.

The beast has no knowledge of cities, cannot even grasp the concept, but it understands that lights along the river's shoreline after sundown mean proximity to areas where prey is plentiful and easy to secure. It recognizes food by shape and size, by scents that dead or living bodies transmit on the river's current, and it has a taste for both.

The scent it favors most is that of blood.

The predator exists outside of time, entirely ignorant of how long it has lived, where it was born, or how it was conceived. If it could understand such things—a physical impossibility—it would not care.

It lives to feed, digest and defecate, without regard for anything around it that cannot be killed and eaten, or else swept aside by its prodigious girth and weight. An urge to procreate occasionally roils its brain, but forays up and down the river, even past New Orleans to the larger Gulf of Mexico, have failed to turn up a potential mate.

And once that futile mating urge has passed away, decreasing in its frequency of late, the animal's age-old imperative would always reassert itself.

Seek. Find. Annihilate. Devour.

Simple.

It was not wholly insensate, even so.

The creature felt alarm from time to time, although few other river denizens could match its size or sheer ferocity. Granted, there *were* some larger than itself, but they were sluggish, maybe blind and deaf, more likely to inflict an injury upon the hunter by colliding with it, rending flesh and crushing bones with no seeming awareness that their paths had intersected.

After several encounters left its thick hide scarred, the predator had learned how to avoid those heedless enemies.

More recently, it had discovered how to stop them, render them helpless, and feed upon them lived aboard the river's juggernauts.

Such tasty meat, but rarely satisfying to the hunter's stomach on a small scale.

In conjunction with built-in alarms that warned the beast of imminent danger, it also felt a certain basic curiosity. When it was safe, the beast surfaced in darkness to observe bright lights ashore. Its ears, though rudimentary and more amendable to picking up vibrations underwater, also registered peculiar noises in the open air above.

Last night was an example, though the beast could not sense passing time aside from noting whether darkness or daylight prevailed over its world. It had been swimming slowly southward, rising to the surface for a long, deep breath of humid air to fill its lungs, when two explosive sounds rang out and echoed over open water like small thunderclaps.

They were not thunder, which the beast perceived as a prolonged cacophony of sound, accompanied by jagged bolts of light that rent the sky and left a burnt sensation on the breeze, as from a distant fire.

What did the jolting sounds portend? Without a grasp of past or future, living solely in the moment, the great beast knew only that their racket posed no threat. In bygone times, it had detected louder sounds along the river, some that stung its ears, others that scattered brilliant lights across the nighttime sky.

It knew nothing of wars or celebrations, could no more distinguish cannon fire from Roman candles sent aloft on holidays. The silent swimmer lived on primitive sensations: heat and cold, bland weather versus storms, hunger experienced and satisfied, pleasure and pain.

And of them all, hunger always prevailed.

Giving a strong flick of its tail, the beast surged forward, staying mostly out of sight beneath the Mississippi's surface unless required to take another breath.

It craved fresh meat and would not be denied.

SILVER STREET, NATCHEZ

Breakfast was plentiful and adequate. Thorn cleaned his plate and paid his tab, leaving a fifty-cent piece for the waitress who had barely spoken to him and who seemed embarrassed to receive any gratuity. He stepped outside and held the door ajar just long enough to hear the conversation of his fellow diners grow in volume once they figured he was out of earshot.

Thorn was passing by an alley on his way back to the Haverstock Hilltop, when someone lurking in the shadows hissed at him.

"Pssst!"

He half turned, both hands dipping toward his twin

Colts, when a slender white man showed himself with empty palms raised shoulder high.

"I ain't heeled," he declared.

Thorn glanced each way across the street, then stepped into the alley, asking, "Who are you and what's your business?"

"Fuller Walsh," the stranger said. "A friend sent me to find you at the Hilltop, but the clerk told me you'd gone for breakfast somewhere."

"And your friend's name is...?"

"Erasmus Finch."

Thorn knew that any of the whitecap raiders from last night could know the freedman's name, thinking that it would be an easy way to gull him, trying to establish confidence between them. Gideon could see no weapon showing, but he didn't feel like taking any chances, either.

"Turn around and lift your jacket up in back," he ordered. "Any sudden moves could your last."

Walsh did as he was told, leaving his back to Thorn and asking, "Are you satisfied?"

"For now," Gideon said, as Walsh turned back to facc him.

"What's the message?" Thorn inquired.

He knew what it *should* be, but an opponent using Finch's name to trick him should be clueless.

"Are you sure you wanna talk about it here?" Walsh asked.

"I'm sure I want an answer P.D.Q."

"Okay, then. It's about my submarine."

"Yours?"

"Mine and Finch's. I'm the one what found it, but we salvaged it together."

"How would that work, in a place like this?"

"You mean the color bar?" Walsh shrugged. "Me and Erasmus have been friends since we were little nippers, way before the war. My folks were always ragging me to stay away from 'im, and likely his people the same, I've got trouble listening to hog slop I don't see no reason for."

"You know I spoke to Mr. Finch last night," Thorn said.

"And nearly got him killed. He isn't holding that against you, so I reckon I won't either."

"So, you have the gist of our discussion, then?"

"The damned thing some are saying plies the river, eating men. Erasmus has his mind made up it got his cousin outa Vidalia."

"What do you think about his plan for getting rid of it?" Thorn asked.

"Can't rightly say, not knowing what we might be up against."

That *we* again. But how far could Thorn trust it?

"Did you plan on helping?" he asked Walsh.

"I might. Been outa work a while and money's getting tight. Maybe this damned what-is-it thing can turn a dollar for us if we put it on display or something. Ain't had time to really think it through."

That sounded honest, anyway.

"Suppose we find it," Thorn said. "Let's assume it's dangerous."

"Must be," Walsh said, "if it could wreck the *Faust* and gobble sailors down."

"Would you still want to come along?"

"It ain't my notion of a party, but why not? I haven't got a lot to lose. And anyhow, you won't get anywhere without me."

"Oh? Why's that?"

"We have the boat you need, but I'm the only one can run it."

"Care to fill me in on that?"

"I'm glad you asked," Walsh answered, smiling. "I was one of 'em what operated it during the war."

THE BRASS RAIL TAVERN

Yancy Olson sat across from Chief Hightower in a backroom of the tavern, closed off to its normal customers.

There were a few of those already drinking in the main barroom, and never mind the early hour. When a man got twitchy and he didn't have a paying job to do, if he had ten cents in his pocket, he could slake his thirst at any time of day or night.

Natchez was good to its inhabitants and visitors that way.

Olson was working on his second glass of whiskey, eyes downcast, worried by Chief Hightower's baleful glare.

"You let me down last night," Hightower said. "You disappointed everyone who matters in the county, and they've tossed that back on me."

"That goddamn Yankee got the drop on us while we's calling the nigger out," Olson replied, and hoped it didn't sound like he was whining. "Then both of 'em started shooting at us, with a rifle and a scattergun."

"How of you were there?" asked Hightower.

"Seven, counting me."

"And all of you were armed."

Not sounding like a question, then, but Olson answered anyhow. "O' course."

"How many of your fired?"

"Um..."

"What's the matter? Was there so much shooting that you couldn't keep track of it?"

"Chief, you gotta understand—"

"Did you get off a single round? Did *anyone*?"

Yancy could see no good to come from lying at that point. "No, sir," he said.

"No, sir! The lot of you were too damn scared to fight back. Not one shot from seven of you, packing who knows how much iron. All running for your lives like pickaninnies."

"Chief, they shot at couple of us!"

"Missed you, didn't they? Were you up front and leading, or back hiding in the woods?"

"Up front," said Yancy. That was true, at least, for all the good it did.

"They just decided to ignore you?"

"How 'n hell do I know what they had in mind?"

"You would've felt bullets and buckshot passing by you, right?"

"Well..."

"But all you come away with was a slug in Orley Utter's shoulder," said Hightower, "and a graze on Davey Vinton's scalp, likely won't even leave a scar."

Davey was Elwood's younger brother and a useless tagalong in Olson's view, but once you let one sibling in, how did you tell another that he couldn't join?

"Maybe we should've took more men."

"Remind me who the leader is," Hightower said.

"That's me, Chief."

"Speak up, damn your eyes! I can't hear you!"

"I am!"

"You're goddamn right. So, it was *your* choice of how

many boys you took along and how you laid your plans. Nobody else."

"No, sir."

"And now I'm in the muck because of you."

"Who's blaming you, Chief?"

"Who? Well, let me see. How 'bout the men who say whether I keep my badge or get my ass run outa town? Don't tell me that I need to list their names."

"No, sir."

"They're blaming me because I let a numskull try 'n do a man's job, when I should've known he couldn't get it done. Is it becoming any clearer to you now?"

"You wanna set a meeting up, Chief, I could tell 'em that it weren't your fault."

Hightower barked a laugh at that. "You think they'd meet with *you*? Walk up and shake your hand like you were something more than poor white trash?"

"Now, Chief—"

"Now, what?"

"Nothing."

"That's what I thought. Now listen up and listen hard. You've got one chance and only one to fix this mess you made."

"What should I do?"

"You're asking me?"

"Well..."

"This damned Yankee has a bunch of lawyers back in Boston, and they know the governor. They know more people even farther up the ladder. Understand?"

"Farther up?"

"Let's say their high enough to bring the bluecoats back if something happens to 'im."

"So—"

"That's if something was *seen* to happen, Yancy. On the other hand, if he just up and left, took off without a word to anybody...well, who knows? They can't hold anyone responsible for that, do you imagine?"

"No?"

"Hell, no. And if he's never seen again, if there's no trace of 'im in Adams County, what am I or anybody else supposed to do about it?"

"Nothing I can think of, Chief."

"For once, you're thinking right."

"I hate to ask," said Yancy, screwing up his courage, "but if something should go wrong that weren't my fault..."

"If anything goes wrong, no one comes back," Hightower said. "Die trying, like a squad of soldiers should."

NINE

FOUR MILES NORTHEAST OF NATCHEZ

"So, how much farther?" Thorn asked Fuller Walsh.

Mounted on an aged bay roan gelding, Walsh said, "Just another hundred, maybe hundred fifty yards, back in the woods."

"Seems like an odd place for a submarine."

"That's by design. Last place you'd look, if they imagined that the *Sturgeon* wasn't shelled and sunk."

"That's what you call it?"

"Yessir. She was christened CSS *Sturgeon*, but I doubt that the South is gonna rise again."

"If you don't mind me saying so," Thorn interjected, "that seems out of character."

"What does?"

"You being lifelong friends with Mr. Finch but fighting on the side of slavery."

"I didn't have no choice," Walsh said. "The First Conscription Act of April 1862 drafted all able-bodied men between the ages of eighteen and thirty-five. Year after that, Congress packed with wealthy planters turned around and passed their Twenty-Slave Law that you might have heard about."

"Exempting any white man who owned twenty slaves or more from military service," Gideon filled in, remembering his history from Harvard.

"That's it. If there was any doubt about secession and the war that sprung from it being a rich man's game, it died right there."

"But you stayed on in uniform."

"Deserting would've put me up before a firing squad," Walsh said. "Besides, once they'd assigned me to the *Sturgeon*, I imagined that I'd never get a shot off toward the Yankees. And it turns out I was right."

"How did you manage to get hold of it after the cease-fire?" Thorn inquired.

"I'll tell you that bit later, if there's time. Right now, we're here."

In front of them, an old barn had collapsed in ruins, overgrown by weeds and vines. Its once-red paint had faded over time to an anemic pink. Its sagging roof was open to the sky above, a yellow slash pine sprouting from its ruptured roof and overshadowed the wreckage. Seasons past had strewn the swaybacked roof with castoff needles, mostly brown now, so that any shingles left were nicely camouflaged.

Outside the barn, in front of buckled double doors, Erasmus Finch was waiting with his mule and sawed-off scattergun.

"Looks like you made it through the night all right," Thorn said.

"Caddie ain't happy with me, but she only is 'bout half the time, no matter what."

A lifelong bachelor, Thorn offered no reply to that. Instead, he asked his two companions, "So, your submarine's in there?"

"Best place to hide it," Finch said. "Set back from the river and no reason to believe that anything's inside. Even coon hunters wouldn't bother breaking in, for fear the roof might come down on their heads."

"I had the same thought," Gideon admitted.

"Wait until you get a look inside," Walsh said. "You're in for a surprise."

"Seems like a full day's work, right there," said Thorn.

"Not quite," Finch said. "Most of them weeds are like the makeup on a fancy gal. They cover up a lot and only show what's meant for you to see."

"And what's the trick to getting in?" Thorn asked.

"No trick," Finch said. "Just elbow grease."

With that, he walked around his saddled mule and drew a broad-bladed machete from its sheath beside the shotgun's saddle boot. The chopper's blade had spots of rust along its length, but Thorn saw that its cutting edge was brightly and newly honed.

"Just have to clear the way a bit, then open up these doors," Finch said.

"I didn't think to bring a scythe," said Thorn.

"Don't need one. This'll do the job. Ten minutes give or take, and we should be inside."

In fact, it took less time than that. When Finch had finished, Thorn joined him and Walsh in opening the old barn's double doors. They had to lift and strain a bit, but not that much, and once the doors began to move their hinges proved to be well oiled.

Finch entered first and lit a lantern hanging just inside. Its light drove back the barn's interior shadows, disturbing bats that roosted in its rafters. Over and above their squeaking, Thorn heard silent signals of alarm and tried his best to sooth them with advice that they were not in any danger.

While the barn appeared decrepit from the outside, near total collapse, stout beams had been positioned on the inside to prevent its roof from sagging any farther, and to stop its walls from falling inward. At the center of a spacious room, dusty and draped in cobwebs, a farm wagon stood beneath an oblong shape shrouded in spider webs and dusty canvas. At a glance, Thorn made it thirty-odd feet long and five-foot something tall.

Finch caught him frowning at the present they were going to unwarp and said, "Come on. You ain't seen nothing yet,"

NATCHEZ & NEW ORLEANS LINE HEADQUARTERS

Armond Joslin had not been expecting visitors. When his secretary, Margaret Duchamp, announced that Noah Dearborn had arrived with no appointment, saying he had urgent business to discuss, Joslin almost refused to see him, but on second thought decided that civility required him to play host and make the best of it.

Despite his personal distaste for Noah, Dearborn's River City Bank was still the largest bank in Natchez and one pillar of the town's economy.

The others two were cotton farming and the shipping line Joslin controlled.

Margaret ushered Dearborn in and Joslin faced him with the desk between them, Armond standing with his jacket off, thumbs hooked behind his red suspenders, making no attempt to walk around and shake the banker's hand.

He did not think of Noah as an enemy, but Dearborn's vigorous support fort white supremacy left a bad taste in Joslin's mouth. For his part, Armond had loaned money to black farmers facing bank foreclosure on what little land they owned after the war, and Noah made no secret of resenting it, aiming to boot them off the farms they worked for small yearly returns and sell the land to pampered whites who treated dominance of Nature as their personal God-given right.

"I'm glad you could spare time to see me," Dearborn said.

"Not much though, I'm afraid," Joslin advised. "More meetings coming up."

"Would one of those be with a certain visitor from Boston?"

"As a rule, I don't discuss my customers."

"Ah. So, he's shipping cargo now? I thought he only hunted bogeymen."

"What did you need to talk about, Noah?"

"The reputation of our city," Dearborn answered.

"Like the shooting out on Cottonwood last night?"

"I don't know anything about that."

"Still, it looks bad in the paper, whitecaps running. I mean, since you're concerned about what people think of Natchez."

"Speaking or the *Independent*, have you seen this morning's front-page feature?"

Joslin had devoured it first thing, but now said, "I've been going over paperwork. I'll likely read it later."

"All about our 'river monster' and the man in black who thinks he's Captain Ahab."

Joslin caught the reference to *Moby-Dick*, a whaling novel published twenty-six years earlier to mixed reviews, now out of print and rated a commercial failure.

"I haven't read the book," he answered honestly.

"No need. Your Mr. Thorn—"

"Not *mine*, Noah."

Dearborn ignored the interruption and pressed on. "He seems to think our river is a nest of monsters. Every time the story's told, it grows a little wilder. Have you heard the claims a giant serpent sank the *Faust*?"

"We still don't know what happened there," Armond replied.

"And now, I understand he's pestering the one man who survived, your ex-employee."

"No one's fired him that I know of," Joslin countered.

"What I hear, Thorn's trying to support the drunkard's fairy tale."

"Nothing suggests the mate was drinking when it happened."

"Even so. You don't believe this superstitious tripe, do you? Please tell me that you don't, Armond."

"I'm waiting to see evidence, whichever way it goes."

"Commendable, I'm sure. But in the meantime, surely you must see it's in the city's best interest to nip these rumors in the bud."

"Most rumors die out on their own, I find," Joslin replied.

"Still, trumpeting them in the *Independent* can't do Natchez any good. Can we at least agree on that?"

"The only thing I have to do with Jubal's paper is the weekly advertisements that he runs for me."

"And that's exactly why I'm here," Dearborn replied. "Until Kenfield comes to his senses, I'm encouraging readers to cancel their subscriptions and his advertisers to withdraw their copy."

"What about the First Amendment, Noah?"

"Do you think the Constitution's authors wanted freedom of the press for scandal sheets and lies?"

"I wouldn't know," Joslin replied. "They had their lapses, though, including the three-fifths clause."

Color rising in his cheeks, Dearborn fired back. "You think it was unreasonable that state populations were allowed to count some of their slaves as residents for purposes of winning seats in Congress?"

"When the Negroes couldn't vote, weren't citizens, and had no say over their lives? I'd say that went beyond unreasonable, into shameful."

Dearborn swallowed hard. Replied, "In that case, I'm surprised you still do so much business with the River City Bank."

"It's funny you should say that, Noah. When you barged in here, I was considering if I should pull out my accounts and start a new bank of my own. Maybe invite colored depositors and welcome their investments in my shipping line."

"You're sounding dangerously like a nigger-lover, Armond."

"I suppose I could apologize for disappointing you," said Joslin, "but the fact is I don't give a damn. Now, if we're finished here...?"

"I'd say that sums it up," Dearborn replied.

"When you get back to work, start on the paperwork to

close out my accounts. And watch those numbers, Noah. I have records of them to the penny."

COTTONWOOD ROAD

"Nobody home," Dwight Peckham told his fellow white-caps, as he stepped out of the shotgun shack.

"We *see* that," Yancy Olson told him, while the others cursed and muttered.

Not like it was any great surprise, thought Olson, scowling underneath his flour sack where no one else could see him.

There'd been no lamps burning when they rode up to surround the place, no sound of anybody running out the back to get away, and no uppity darky with a shotgun coming out to stare them down like on their visit.

Erasmus Finch was gone, along with anybody else who had been lodging with him.

"Anybody know where he might run to?" Yancy asked his men. "Has he got any family?"

"Who knows?" One of them answered back.

"Should ask his overseer," someone else advised.

"No good," Olson replied. "I checked on that first thing. Ain't had no job to speak of since the war. Just lives by hand to mouth, odd jobs and such."

"Somebody should've run him off back then," another groused.

"Somebody didn't, though," said Olson. "Hush a minute now and let me think."

It didn't take a minute, though, for Yancy to decide what should be done.

"Until we find 'im," he announced, "I wanna make damn sure he don't come back here. Light it up!"

That made a couple of the whitecaps whoop and holler as they climbed down from their horses, being careful with the torches they had stopped to light on their ride out from town. Two pitched their firebrands through the open doorway, one more busting out a window, and a fourth tossing his flame onto the hovel's roof.

In nothing flat, the shabby house was blazing from its floor up to the rafters, pouring smoke out of its door and windows, more curling from underneath the eaves. For just a heartbeat, Yancy wished they'd shot it up instead, but that would have meant wasting shot and powder when they wouldn't stop Finch or some other shiftless character from moving in and patching up the bullet holes.

This way, at least, if someone wanted to reoccupy the homesite they would have to start from scratch, and it would take a while—during which time the whitecaps could return and light another bonfire underneath the stars.

Radiant heat from the collapsing structure drove back men and horses to a distance they could tolerate. From there, they sat and watched the wreck burn down to glowing coals before they turned away and started back to Natchez.

Leading them, although he had accomplished something, Olson knew that Chief Hightower wasn't going to be satisfied. His final words to Yancy echoed like a death knell inside Olson's head.

If anything goes wrong, no one comes back. Die trying, like a squad of soldiers should.

Some of the boys were laughing, joshing with each other, and he snapped at them to cut short their frivolity.

"We ain't done yet," he told them. "Still got more places

to check before we knock off for the night. Maybe we'll find 'im yet."

"And if we don't?" one hooded rider asked. "What then?"

"We still got work to finish up in town," Yancy replied.

If he had raised his mask just then, the others could have seen him smile.

FOUR MILES NORTHEAST OF NATCHEZ

When Finch and Walsh removed the tarpaulin, Gideon had his first view of their submarine.

The *Sturgeon* was some twenty-five or twenty-six feet long, a tube that tapered at both ends to simulate a large hand-rolled cigar. Its bow or nose was pointed toward the barn's exit, still bearing faded traces of its painted name, nearly illegible today. Two screws protruded from the stern above a rudder roughly four feet square.

The whole thing was constructed out of iron, with rivets showing where its curved plates were attached. Along its topside length, a bulge Thorn took for added headspace ran along some two-thirds of the submersible's full length. On top and to the rear, a trapdoor lay flush with the upper deck, no latch apparent from outside.

Thorn pointed to it. Asked, "That latches from inside?"

"For safety's sake," Walsh said. "The crew can get out if they need to."

"If they can," Finch interjected.

"And what's this?" Gideon asked them, pointing toward a three-foot-long protuberance on top, located toward the nose.

"A lookout tube with mirrors in it," Walsh said. "Let's you watch what's going on topside while running underwater. Fella who invented it called it a 'polemoscope.' Try making sense of that."

"Three men can fit inside there?" Gideon inquired.

"It's tight, but yeah," Walsh said. "The first one in handles the scope and the torpedo. Middleman hand-cranks the screws. Last guy in line controls the rudder, taking his directions from the one up front."

"No leaks?" Thorn asked.

"You get some condensation on the inside when its under," Finch said. "Puddles down around your backside, but the seals were good last time we took it out."

"And when was that?" asked Gideon.

"About six months ago," said Walsh.

"We don't go out in daytime," Finch amended. "Too much chance of being seen."

"You mentioned a torpedo," Thorn reminded them.

"We got a couple of 'em over here," Finch said, and led him toward the sagging barn's north wall, where two long poles stood upright in a corner, wrapped in more canvas.

Walsh pulled it back just far enough for Gideon to see smooth wooden shafts, each ending with a barbed spear tip set forward of a bulky metal cylinder.

"How do you use it? Thorn asked.

"It attaches to the *Sturgeon*'s prow and juts out forward. When you ram a target, if it's got a wooden hull, the spear sticks and you back away, reversing the direction of your screws. That long cord hanging down attaches to a ring outside the *Sturgeon*'s hull and trails behind you as you back away. Get to the end of it, the submarine's weight draws it taut, pulls a spring-loaded trigger patterned on an old flintlock, and that sets off the chare."

"With any luck," Finch added. "No one's tried it in a

dozen years, at least. We keep the trigger oiled up nice, but whether it'll blow, well..."

Thorn nodded. Asked them, "So, who's up for a trial run?"

"What?" Walsh said

"You mean right now?" Finch asked.

"Unless you've got a better time in mind," Thorn said.

Step one involved hitching up Walsh's horse and Finch's mule to draw the creaking wagon from the barn and down a pair of grassy ruts to reach the Mississippi's bank. They left the spar torpedoes in the barn and closed its double doors after they got the wagon clear.

When they had reached the Mississippi's edge, a cove shielded by mossy cypress trees on to north and south, Thorn's two companions rustled up the pieced of a wooden ramp that had been tossed around to look like scrap wood, getting them arranged to form a slide that that stopped a few feet short of contact with the inlet's water.

Next, they attached tow ropes to iron rings welded in a circle near the *Sturgeon*'s nose. Empty, the submarine weighed less than Thorn expected, some four hundred pounds. Its rudder folded up to keep from dragging on the ground, and with some help from Shadow—mentally protesting all the way—they dragged it to the water's edge.

Again, Thorn was surprised to note its buoyancy, remaining upright in the water thanks to wedge-shaped fins mounted above the midline of its hull. Walsh used a small handle to raise the stern's trapdoor and crawled inside, followed by Gideon, with Finch being the last in line.

If Thorn had ever fallen prey to claustrophobia, it would

have been too much for him, but as he settled on a thinly padded seat and found the handle that controlled the *Sturgeon*'s rudder, he relaxed.

Behind him, Finch secured the entry hatch and gave the submarine's twin screws a slow twist, nudging them into the Mississippi's flow. From there, the *Sturgeon*'s weight submerged them, leaving nothing but its "polemoscope" showing above the surface. Thorn watched Walsh, seated in front of him, and swung the rudder's handle left or right according to their pilot's orders.

"How long can we stay submerged?" he asked.

"The scope comes with an air tube welded to it," Walsh explained. "It ain't like strolling through a meadow, but unless we sink down and the tube starts sucking water, we can breathe all right."

"No worse than working in a coal mine," Finch chimed in.

Until the shaft caves in, Gideon thought, but kept that to himself.

While they were cruising slowly underwater, Fuller Walsh watching for surface craft and other obstacles, Thorn set his mind adrift. He'd never managed mental contact with a fish but thought it couldn't hurt to try, in case their quarry was somewhere in the vicinity and was descended from some line of creatures open to communication.

It was no surprise when he got nothing, but it helped to pass the time, while perspiration beaded on his forehead and tickled beneath his arms. He had expected to feel cold inside the submarine, but it was just the opposite, three bodies packed inside, their breath beginning to grow stale by slow degrees.

"This good enough for now?" Walsh asked, half turning from the scope that guided them.

"Suits me," Thorn said.

"Okay, then. Crank the rudder hard left for the turning back to shore."

Only a test, so far.

The next time they went out, hunting for real, Thorn wondered what might lie in wait for them.

TEN

NATCHEZ

Thorn returned in time to stable Shadow, brushing down the stallion and spending some time with Belle before he stashed his Winchester in his hotel room, then walked down to Pepper Jack's for supper.

Yet another waitress that he'd never seen before came up to greet him on arrival. This one was a redhead with a light dusting of freckles on her cheeks who flashed a pearly smile at Thorn and led him to the window table he'd begun to think of as his usual. He ordered pork chops, mashed potatoes, red-eye gravy and a side of collard greens that proved to be delicious, grilled with spices that enhanced their normal flavor without overwhelming it. Black coffee and a slice of fresh-baked apple pie finished the meal, while other diners spent a bit less time covertly watching him than on his other visits to the restaurant.

Natchez had claimed nine thousand residents at the last census, seven years before, but from his research on the city, Thorn knew that its population was declining, the reputed experts up in Washington, D.C. predicting numbers twenty-odd percent below the last head count when 1880 rolled around. Regardless of the final numbers or the reasons for that exodus, Gideon guessed that most adult Natchezians had heard about his mission now, or knew his name at least, from word of mouth or Jubal Kenfield's writing in the *Independent.*

As to what they thought of him, he had already polled the whitecap vote and wouldn't be surprised if they rebounded from their first humiliation with another bid to run him out of town or worse. He was prepared for that, and had no fear of Chief Hightower's coppers, but expected they would be no help to him if further trouble came his way.

Business as usual for Thorn as locals frequently preferred sweeping their secrets underneath the nearest handy rug, along with anyone who ventured to expose them.

From Pepper Jack's he strolled on to the Brass Rail Tavern, pushed in through the batwing doors, and was enveloped by the same player piano's tinny music that he'd heard last time around. There was no sign of Jubal Kenfield in the barroom, nor of anybody else Thorn recognized, and while he caught some sidelong glances in passing, none of them seemed overtly hostile.

Maybe that would change as those around him downed more alcohol, but Gideon had no plans of remaining longer than it took to quaff a beer and pay his tab.

Bartenders quickly learn that smiles attract more tips than frowns do, the young man serving drinks nodded to Gideon as if he were a long-lost friend. He brought a frosty mug of beer, accepted Thorn's coins with a simple thank-you, and moved on to deal with other customers.

Thorn wasn't sold on using the wartime submersible preserved by Finch and Walsh to hunt the creature he'd some looking for in Adams County. Having tested it himself and tried its "polemoscope" after the *Sturgeon* was securely back inside its barn, he understood the built-in drawbacks.

First, as submarines existed in the present day, they were designed for stalking surface ships and had no means of spotting wildlife underwater, whether large or small. Beyond that, while the *Sturgeon*'s spar torpedo might prove lethal to a living creature, the same problem remained concerning underwater visibility. Beyond that, he could not expect a swimming thing of any size to move predictably and on a steady course, as if it were a warship or a cargo barge.

His failed attempt at mental contact with the creature told Thorn nothing. Distance or distraction could have interfered, or else, whatever the thing proved to be might be another species physically impervious to his odd talent. His knowledge of the entity, whatever it might be, had gained nothing of import since he first arrived in Natchez.

It was large, powerful, dangerous. Beyond that, only mocking question marks remained.

And finally, he had the vessel's two-man crew to think about. They might seem willing to pursue Thorn's prey while it was theoretical—would likely even claim they were committed to the quest—but that could change in seconds flat if they were suddenly confronted by a monster beyond their imaginations.

If one of them panicked underwater, when the chips were down, it could mean death for all aboard.

All that, and Thorn still didn't have a clue how they could find the thing he sought, much less what it would finally turn out to be, how large in fact, or its defensive capabilities.

If it could wreck the *Faust*, how would a small craft like the *Sturgeon* fare?

Tired of considering the negatives this Friday night, Gideon finished off his beer and started back toward his hotel.

SILVER STREET

Hiding in the shadows of an alleyway between a lawyer's office and a bookstore, Yancy Olson watched the black-clad man from Boston drawing closer to the Haverstock Hilltop hotel. He seethed with hatred for the carpetbagger who had faced him down last night and made Yancy a laughingstock among his fellow residents of Natchez.

Well, among the white men, anyhow. They were the only ones who counted in his estimation, and particularly those in power who relied upon the whitecaps to perform their dirty work in times of need.

Yancy was not an educated man—had quit school halfway through fourth grade, in fact—but he was smart enough to know that even when his rich societal superiors regarded him as poor white trash, they still relied upon him and rewarded him for handling jobs they feared to do themselves.

Rather, they *had* relied on Olson until last night, when a Yankee interloper and an uppity black man who'd lost track of his place put Olson and his robed brethren to flight and wounded two of them.

The next worst thing, in Yancy's mind, was being lambasted by Chief Hightower as if he, Yancy, was both a coward and a traitor to his race. Without his reputation as a leader of the whitecaps, standing ever ready to maintain the rigid color bar, Olson had little else in life.

Correction. Make that *nothing* else.

White skin—well, tan, to be precisely accurate—was all that he had going for him, setting him apart from Dixie's darker servile class. The men who gave him orders might be smarter and were damn sure richer than Olson would ever be, but till last night, he'd been a useful tool or weapon hauled out for emergencies.

And in the Mississippi Delta, such emergencies were seldom out of mind, appearing when you least expected them.

In order to regain trust and respect, Yancy had struck upon a plan that he considered bold and relatively foolproof. He had half a dozen whitecaps stationed along Silver Street, surrounding Thorn's hotel and waiting for his signal to close in. His second in command tonight was Elwood Vinton, not the smartest man he'd ever met but hellbent on avenging younger brother Davey's minor injury from their first meeting with the man in black.

All six were armed with pistols, as before, some of them also packing knives, perhaps a couple of them knuckledusters if the fight went hand-to-hand. In that case, Yancy reckoned he would have to join the fray himself, and it humiliated him to realize that he was frightened to his core.

No one must ever know that, come what may.

Not even if it meant his death.

Thorn was thirty paces from his hotel when the shooting started.

First, it was a single pistol shot, hasty and scarcely aimed at all, missing him by at least a yard and shattering the window of a clothing store he'd just passed by. A second shot, from somewhere else, proved equally inept, chipping the Haverstock Hilltop hotel's brickwork in front of him.

Bad shooting, but his adversaries had him bracketed and Thorn decided against running on toward his hotel as he drew both Colt Peacemakers and cocked their hammers. Closer refuge beckoned from an alleyway behind and to his left, its darkness offering concealment.

But the shadows harbored dangers, too.

As Thorn entered the alley, someone there ahead of him rasped out a curse and fired a pistol at close range. He felt the hot wind of a bullet singe his ear, deafened by artificial thunder, nearly blinded by the muzzle flash.

That didn't stop him firing off his left-hand Colt, rewarded by the sound of lead impacting flesh and bone, his adversary crumpling the ground while Gideon closed in and kicked a smoking six-gun from his dying hand.

One down. How many yet to go?

The shooters would be whitecaps, almost certainly. Not that identity was paramount just now, but knowing who his adversaries were, after he'd faced some down last night, gave Thorn an estimate of their intelligence and natural ability.

Of course, even a dimwit might get lucky with a stray shot in the heat of battle.

Risking a glance beyond the alley's mouth, he counted four more shooters at the very least. All were across the street from Thorn's hotel and where he sheltered now, but he assumed there would be others on his side of Silver Street besides the one he'd dropped.

Poor odds, but still not insurmountable.

Along the street, Thorn heard excited voices raised,

both male and female. Back in the direction of the Brass Rail Tavern, men were jabbering and shouting questions, but none of them seemed inclined to venture any closer for a better look at what was happening.

Among sensible men, even if they were three sheets to the wind or getting there, survival trumped mere curiosity.

Thorn waited in the alley, knowing that police must soon arrive in answer to the gunfire, but he wasn't sure which side they might support. He knew from recent history that southern lawmen had collaborated with the KKK and similar secret societies in contravening Reconstruction and defeating efforts to invest freedmen with anything resembling civil rights. The flipside of that coin was Gideon's success in backing down Chief Hightower last night, but even that could prove to be a two-edged sword.

If someone picked off Thorn tonight, the chief could wash his hands of it and blame the crime on unknown perpetrators still at large, feeling no great pressure to solve the case.

Which reinforced Thorn's need to stand up for himself.

He watched the street, did not return the probing fire from pistols on the other side. A minute passed, then two, before his would-be slayers tired of wasting powder on a mark they couldn't see and ventured out to find a better vantage point.

Two gunmen, neither one disguised except for handkerchiefs knotted around their lower faces, came at him from two directions simultaneously, one emerging from the recessed doorway of an office to his left, or north, the other stepping from alley to Thorn's right, midway between him and the Brass Rail Tavern. Both advanced with pistols raised, holding their fire against the moment when Gideon was revealed.

He knew that whether potting wither one before the other would allow the second man—and others of the company besides, still hidden—to return fire with a greater likelihood of hitting him. Thorn had to concentrate, coordinate his movements, and be certain of his aim.

As much as possible, that was.

He cocked his right-hand Peacemaker, linked up his first shot from the shadows, still unseen by the attack on that side. The Single Action Army model's sights were rudimentary and seldom used, a rear notch with a groove extending down the frame above its cylinder, matching a low blade set back half an inch behind the barrel's business end. Gideon barely noticed them as he squeezed off, absorbed the six-gun's recoil, then swung back to find the moving target on his left.

He did not see the first man fall, but heard his bullet strike, a punctured lung expelling pent-up air, and then his eyes were on the second threat, the pistol cocked again and bucking in his hand almost before Thorn found his mark. He targeted the upper chest, was satisfied with thirteen grams of lead drilling his adversary's throat instead, pitching him over on his back.

A ruptured trachea meant no air taken in, no oxygen reaching other gunman's brain or his extremities. Death followed swiftly, whether from blood loss or strangulation.

It was all the same to Thorn.

A last wild shot echoed across the width of Silver Street, and then he heard the gunmen who were still alive and whole running away. At the same time, police were coming down the street from City Hall's direction, Chief Hightower shouting down the thoroughfare, demanding to know what in hell was going on.

Thorn waited for them, holstered both warm Colts,

then rolled the dice by stepping from his hideaway, hands raised to shoulder height.

MIDSTREAM, OFFSHORE FROM NATCHEZ

More sharp explosive sounds, the second time within as many days, lured the silent creature to emerge from hiding in the Mississippi's depths. Eyeing the shore in each direction, without know what directions were, it saw nothing to indicate more pyrotechnics it remembered vaguely from days past.

With nothing to observe, it drew a deep breath and submerged once more, swimming against the river's current, waiting to discover if the secret touch would stir its reptile brain again.

The first time, earlier that day with sunlight gleaming from the water's surface, it had been surprised to feel a strange and wholly new sensation on the inside of its massive skull, above and backward from its eyes. The creature did not realize it had a brain in there, or what a brain might do, knew only that it *was* and did not care to be disturbed.

The touch—not that, exactly, but a similar sensation, as when drifting flotsam brushed against its leather hide—had put the massive swimmer on alert. If something unseen was attacking it by means unrecognized, the standard choice of fight or flight was narrowed down by half. And yet, retreating from some maybe danger that it could not see, hear, taste of smell, went against its nature.

The Mississippi's all-time apex predator feared nothing in the sense that fear was understood by men and lesser animals. Short hours earlier it had devoured a six-foot bottom-feeding paddlefish in two swift shearing bites.

Desert had been an alligator gar, still young and only three feet long, weighing the better part of fifty pounds.

The creature knew no scale of size or weight but understood that anything it could dismember with its long jaws and consume was sustenance. The river's larger denizens, some many times the swimmer's length and fighting weight, were dangerous and indigestible. The only point in rushing after them was a sensation that the creature could not recognize as pleasure.

If the silent touch should come again, the beast would make a sluggish effort to identify it, probably in vain. But if it could connect that feeling to a living creature anywhere within its reach, it knew precisely what to do.

An enemy consumed became no enemy at all.

SILVER STREET

Chief Hightower arrived with gun in hand, red-faced and raging, backed by three policemen marginally larger than himself, all swiveling their heads and spotting dozens of collected witnesses along the street.

One of those on hand, his notebook open, feverishly writing a description of the scene, was Jubal Kenfield from the *Natchez Independent*.

Thorn raised his voice, not shouting, but ensuring that his words carried a block or more to Kenfield and the other avid listeners after the brief firefight.

"Is this going the way you planned it, Chief?" he asked. "It's obvious you want to shoot right now but think it through. Consider all these witnesses who clearly see I'm not resisting you in any way."

Hightower swallowed hard, then managed to reply, "You've killed two Natchez citizens tonight, Mister."

"You've missed one," Thorn corrected him. "He's back here in the alley, where he tried to ambush me. Check all their guns and ask yourself how you'll explain it at the inquest when you try to stand the story on its head."

"I'll take my chances, Yankee."

"That won't help you, Chief. Make a mistake right now, or if you claim I had a fatal 'accident' in jail later, awaiting trial, you'll find yourself without a badge and likely stretching rope. These officers you brought along could end up doing prison time or maybe even climbing up the gallows steps behind you."

Hearing that, the other three policemen started looking worried, on their way toward sickly. One of them spoke up, starting to say, "Uh, Chief—"

"Shut up!" Hightower snapped at him.

But Thorn would not be silenced. Speaking loud and clear, he forged ahead.

"Smart money says these men are whitecaps, Chief. What happens when a prosecutor starts to question them and finds out that you know them all? I've got the basis for subpoenas and a lawsuit as it is. You want to gamble that the federal attorney up in Jackson won't connect you to this set-to?"

"I've done nothing wrong!" Hightower answered back.

Twisting the strict truth of his background slightly, Thorn pressed on.

"Back east I went to Harvard Law School, Chief." Exaggerating there, although he'd *planned* to go before his Aunt Drusilla died. "The Ku Klux Act that Congress passed six years ago prescribes a fine and prison term for anyone who robs another of his rights under color of law. If you don't have a legal dictionary handy, Chief, that means using your badge to punish anyone regardless of their race or politics."

"I ain't afraid of Yankee jail," Hightower blustered.

"Good for you, Chief," Thorn replied, "because you'll definitely wind up in a Yankee jail, so far from home and friends that you'll be the minority of one."

Hightower mulled that over for another moment, then slowly, reluctantly, replaced his six-gun in its holster. Speaking first to one of his three officers, he ordered, "Cletus, run and fetch the undertaker double quick." To Thorn, he growled, "All right. You're free to go, for now, but don't try leaving town."

"I hadn't planned on it," said Gideon, turning away toward his hotel.

As he entered the Haverstock Hilltop, he heard Hightower barking at the other witnesses, "Go on home now, the rest of y'all. There's nothing more to see here. Clear the street."

Another win, Gideon thought, as he passed through the hotel's lobby toward the stairs.

But how long would his luck hold out?

ELEVEN

JUNE 22, 1877

Grover Arquette was an inveterate night-owl who managed to exist on sparse sleep overnight unless he had indulged in too much booze. Given his size and appetites, however, too much liquor for the Democratic Party kingmaker to handle comfortably might have killed a lesser man outright.

As Friday turned the corner into Saturday, Arquette could barely feel the shots of Irish whiskey he had put away. What he *did* feel, instead, was escalating fury toward the town's chief of police.

"Shut up, Hal!" he commanded, when Chief Hightower was barely halfway through his recitation of the night's events.

"Yes, sir," the chief replied, face reddening.

"I need to get this straight before you say another word." Arquette reached out to pour himself another double shot, the chief still high and dry with nothing offered to him. After a burning sip, he forged ahead.

"So, Yancy Olson and his numskulls tried to kill this

Yankee on the street outside the Haverstock Hilltop, but he dropped three of them instead?"

"Yes, sir."

"What happened to the others?"

"Ran away to hide somewhere."

"Including Olson."

"Yes, sir."

"And they did this downtown, in front of *beaucoup* witnesses, because he winged a couple of 'em last night, at some nigger's shack on Cottonwood?"

"The boy's name is Erasmus Finch," Hightower said. "Thorn rode out there to meet with 'im."

"About this river monster some folks are riled up about."

"Yes, sir."

"You didn't toss him in the calaboose for shooting two white men?"

"No, sir. As I explained to you last night—"

"He's got some fancy lawyers back in Boston and they know our governor, along with heaps of folks in Washington."

"Yes, sir."

"I'm with you so far, Hal," Arquette conceded. "Now, explain to me how in pluperfect hell tonight's shindig was *your* idea."

"No, sir! I gotta stop you there. All I told Yancy was to handle it some way that wouldn't boomerang on us."

"Which Olson, ignoramus that he is and always has been, took to mean he might as well turn Silver Street into a shooting gallery?"

"Well..."

Arquette cut him off. "The way I see it, Hal, we've only got two explanations for this damned fiasco. Number one, you gave the order and you're lying now to try and keep your own ass off the griddle."

"No, sir! That ain't true."

"Or number two, you gave some vague instructions to an idiot who turned around and fucked 'em up, and us into the bargain."

"Well..."

"If there's a number three, Hal, this would be the time to spit it out."

Slouching, defeated, in a way that emphasized his paunch, Hightower said, "I guess it's number two."

"And you stepped in a stinking pile of it," Arquette confirmed. "My only question now is how you're gonna clear away this mess you've made."

"I'll talk to Yancy, sir."

"You'll *talk* to him? Correct me if I'm wrong on this, but hasn't *talking* to him done enough damage already?"

"Um..."

" 'Um,' shit! I've got the governor and speaker of the Mississippi House of Representatives both breathing down my neck, wanting to know how *I* let this calamity get outa hand. They're blaming *me* for your mistakes, and I won't have it, Hal. You hear me?"

"Yes, sir."

"So, here's what you do. Get hold of Yancy and that other trash he runs with. Reel 'em in and make damn sure they'll not be telling tales to anybody, ever. Can you handle that, or should I take that badge o' yours and pin it on somebody else?"

"No, sir! I mean, yeah, I can handle that okay."

"I hope so, Hal. If this gets any worse, I'll have to cut the weak links from the daisy-chain myself and you'll be one of 'em. I've worked too long and hard to sacrifice it all for idjits."

"Understood, sir."

"Good. I hope so. Now get outa here and don't come back to me with any more bad news."

THE HAVERSTOCK HILLTOP HOTEL

Gideon Thorn stood at his window, risked it being open and with drapes pulled back, and eyed the midnight river view. Before trying to sleep, he had a plan in mind that might or might not work, but he felt duty-bound to try.

From childhood, Thorn had never fully understood his knack for mentally communicating with various animals. When it happened for the first time, Gideon had feared that he had lost his mind, gone crazy, or that fleeting contact with the beast that massacred his family had managed to infect him somehow, leaving scars upon his psyche as one of its talons had across his scalp.

It was a simple house mouse, one of many rodents dwelling at the orphanage in Lawrence, Kansas Territory, that first spoke to him. Today, from studying zoology at Harvard, Thorn knew that the creature's Latin scientific name was *Mus musculus*, not that it made any difference.

The mouse, of course, had not addressed him as one person speaks to others. While its nose was twitching, Gideon could swear he never saw its lips move, nor had those of any other creatures he'd communed with through the intervening years. The mouse produced no auditory words, but rather touched something inside Thorn's head that tingled faintly and produced the mental image of a question mark.

That evening, and during other contacts over time, he'd

felt the little rodent "asking" who and what he was. Thorn tried to answer back as best he could and felt another strange sensation, as of simple concepts leaping from his brain into the other smaller one. He could determine when the mouse was hungry or when it had lately dined on kitchen scraps. He'd looked forward to their meetings with anticipation, learned to reach out farther to make contact, and had "felt" it for a fleeting instant when a mousetrap crushed his small friend's skull.

As Thorn aged, grew into his unexpected talent, he began to catalog which "lower" species were receptive to communication, which could not be touched at all, and tagged a few who seemed to "hear" him but felt no enticement to respond. He could attract some species or repel them.

Two broad classes that eluded him were human beings and—at least, so far—all bird species. As with the source of his ability, Thorn had no clue why *Homo sapiens* and all members of the feathered subclass *Aves* were impervious to his telepathy.

That didn't matter to him now.

Tonight, despite his failure of that afternoon, he reached out once again in hope of contacting the Mississippi's unknown lurking denizen.

Without knowing what it might be, Thorn recognized his disadvantage. His failure to "connect" that afternoon, while gliding underneath the river's surface with his two companions in the *Sturgeon*, made him question whether he was simply wasting time tonight.

But there were other reasons that he might have missed the creature, whatever it was, with Finch and Walsh on their excursion. Distance, he had learned, affected contact to the point that any organism slipped past Thorn if it was more than half a mile or so away. Besides that, he had no idea whether submersion in water exacerbated interference, of if sitting in a vessel forged from iron prevented thoughts from traveling beyond the *Sturgeon*'s hull.

He saw no clear reason why that should be the case, but even after twenty-odd years of sporadic practice, much about Thorn's covert skill remained obscure to him.

He only knew it couldn't hurt to try again.

His mind reached out, a small *pulling* sensation, as if some fly-fishing sportsman on the far side of the river had had hooked a small part of his brain and then tugged on the line, setting his hook. There was no pain, per se, only a sense of being *stretched* beyond the bony limits of his skull.

Then cold, as if he'd dived into the river, sinking like a stone, achieving buoyancy be slow degrees and with a modicum of effort. Cold shapes brushed against him, sleek and sinuous. Above him, on the surface, Thorn could hear and feel a long flat-bottomed scow passing, while his eyes followed its progress from his hotel window.

No contact with any of the crew aboard, no contact from the Mississippi's depths, until...

Instead of pulling, this time Thorn experienced a *push* against his gray matter, tried to identify its source but only gained impressions of its length and massive weight. If he'd been staring out to sea, he might have thought it was a whale, perhaps half grown, but as it was, in freshwater, he had no frame of reference.

There was a touch, a probe or curiosity, and Thorn tried to respond, delivering an invitation for the creature to reveal itself, his eyes scanning the river's surface as the scow passed on its way to southward.

What was that, visible for a second, maybe two, reflecting light from a three-quarter moon above?

It might have been the scow's wake, nothing more or less, but something in the way it rolled and glimmered with a sheen like dampened leather made him hesitate to write it off so easily.

He sent another probe, not quite a challenge but approaching one, to see if he could make the creature tip its hand. Its *fin*? Would it reveal a bit more of itself, assuming it was even there at all?

A splash rewarded him, which might have been a tail tip's flicking as a large shape dived, or could have been two wakes colliding in midstream, even a fish leaping to snap at insects for a nightly meal.

And it was gone.

Thorn tried again, strained with the effort, then gave up to stop familiar pinpricks he felt stabbing at his temples.

There'd been *something*, though he couldn't pin it down.

And if he'd called it to the surface once, however fleetingly, why not a second time?

THE NATCHEZ INDEPENDENT OFFICE

In all his time printing the *Independent*, Jubal Kenfield had not run an "Extra" after putting out a normal run on Friday morning.

This would be a first for him and for the city that he served.

Of course, they'd never had a full-blown shootout in the heart of town before, despite all manner of ambushes and assassinations during Reconstruction on the city's outskirts and surrounding countryside.

Call that another first—and hopefully the last. Although the way matters were going, Kenfield could not rest assured of that.

Three dead, all likely members of the whitecaps, though he'd be using "alleged," perhaps "reputed" members to avoid lawsuits for defamation. Jubal wasn't sure if any of the whitecaps could have passed for literate, but they had friends in Natchez who could read—some of them highly placed—and who would whisper in their ears about filing a charge of libel if their cowardly masked brotherhood was named without hard proof.

Three dead by Gideon Thorn's hand, and others in the wind after a near-miss with the Grim Reaper. Kenfield doubted that any others would be questioned, much less charged and put on trial, since Anglo-Saxon Mississippi had a blind spot where the crimes of racist vigilantes were concerned. In cases where they heaped too much embarrassment upon their betters, nightriders might be advised to find another town, county or state in which to ply their trade. Those who refused to leave might suffer "accidents" or simply disappear without a trace into the river or the swamps that had devoured so many of their dark-skinned brethren stretching back decades before the Civil War.

And those who fled or shuffled off this mortal coil would be replaced, of course, by others pledged to mind their manners and do only as they were instructed from on high. Another group of terrorists would rise, shoulder their predecessors off the stage, and run roughshod over the county until they, in turn, became too brash and arrogant to live within the shadow of polite society.

Polite to fellow white men, anyway.

Kenfield had not been quick enough to catch Thorn for an interview before he started setting type for an unprecedented Saturday edition, but he'd seen and heard enough after the killings to report it without seeming to take sides. In shorthand, he had captured most of Chief Hightower's words and Thorn's replied nearly verbatim. He could set the scene, described sprawled bodies, then allow the chief antagonists to speak out for themselves.

And now, his work nearly completed, Jubal wondered what might happen next.

Who else might not survive?

MIDSTREAM, OFFSHORE FROM NATCHEZ

The predator was puzzled, but not worried in the sense that humans fret and fume over a situation's possible outcome. It had experienced a sense of being *probed* but had no sense of that feeling's significance, much less considering it as a future risk.

The beast had never previously felt a call to surface and reveal itself. Long years had passed since last it mated with another of its kind, and that had happened far from where it swam tonight. There had been no instinctive primal urge behind the odd sensation, yet it had responded as if driven to comply as surely as it felt compelled to eat and void its waste at cyclic intervals.

A more evolved brain might have wondered when, or if, the call would come again.

And if so, how should it respond?

Did it, in fact, have any choice?

Trying to think sparked hunger in the creature's belly, redirecting its attention to taste and an aroma wafting toward it from upstream. It recognized the source, if not by name, at least by memories of taste and texture. Something vaguely similar—though much, much smaller—than itself. Not quite related, but at least vaguely akin.

The predator's long flattened tail lashed at the south-bound current, surging northward, veering closer to the river's western shore. It knew nothing of states or borders, but it clearly recognized the narrowing proximity of prey.

Despite the Mississippi's murk, its eyes picked out a target closing from its left, another animal for which it had no name. Jaws opened wide, it rushed upon the midsized alligator, catching it behind its right foreleg, long teeth ripping through the smaller reptile's body armor to release a blood and viscera into the monster's mouth.

Two mighty chomps and it was done, the gator's head and still-attached forelegs sinking through crimson swirls, its tail and hindquarters trailing until the spine, sheared through, released them into darkness with the other castoff bits.

Not bad, but still inadequate to satisfy the midnight swimmer.

Its prodigious appetite demanded more, perhaps the unknown creature that had teased its brain brief moments earlier.

If not tonight, then maybe soon.

COTTONWOOD ROAD

Erasmus Finch stood staring at the ashes of his simple home. The blackened rubble still exuded head and fouled the air around him.

"Sorry about your house," said his companion, Fuller Walsh.

"It wasn't much to start with," Finch replied. "I got out most of what we needed when I ran for it."

"How's Caddie holding up? Walsh asked.

"It's nothing that we ain't been through before."

Walsh dropped it there. Despite his on-and-off lifetime of friendship with the black man standing next to him, he knew it was impossible for him to truly understand Finch's experience, much less what all his captive people had endured since their abduction out of Africa, through slavery, the war that never really ended after Appomattox until white men reigned supreme again, and now the legislative landslide that had relegated black folks back to something very much like bondage via sharecropping, chain gangs, and whitecaps riding where the Ku Klux Klan had left off only four or five years earlier.

"Maybe it's best," Walsh ventured, "that we just forget about this other business. Let it go."

"You think so, Fuller?"

"All we gotta do is just stay off the river for a while, until this thing—whatever it turns out to be—gets fed up and moves on to someplace else."

"Just make it someone else's problem, then?"

Walsh shrugged, wishing they could clear out of there, quit staring at the remnants of what struck him as a funeral pyre. "You think about it," he replied, "we won't be making anything of it. We didn't start it, did we?"

"Nope."

"And no one's gonna blame us if takes a little longer finishing its own way, without us pretending we know what we're doing."

"We *do* know," Finch said, correcting him.

"Maybe *you* do. So far, I ain't convinced."

"Since when?"

Walsh started counting on his calloused fingers, raising each in turn to make his points.

"Okay, first thing: we've got no idea what this critter even *is*, except it's hungry all the time and too damn big for us to handle with a three-man submarine."

"You might be wrong on that," Finch said. "In fact, I'm betting that you are."

"All right. Second, we've got nobody on our side except this fancy man from Boston who the whitecaps wanna kill, and us along with 'im. It's bad enough we can't be seen talking together, much less going on some crazy monster hunt."

"Not crazy if it works," Finch countered. "We'd be heroes then."

Walsh snorted laugher. "You been at the 'shine again, Raz? Which white man in charge do you think's ever gonna give us credit for a goddamned thing? You're still a slave in their eyes, and I'm just...well, you know."

"Say it, Fuller. 'Nigger-lover'."

"Don't put words in my mouth when you've never heard me use 'em, Raz."

"I'm right though, and you know it. That's what's got you worried."

"Not the *only* thing," Walsh answered back. "Bad as it gets sometimes, I'd kinda like to stay alive."

"You think I wouldn't?"

"How 'n hell would I know? You take chances when there ain't no need of it."

"What else is life but taking chances?" Finch replied.

"Another question for some other time. Right now, *my* life means catching up on sleep."

Finch nodded. Said, "I'd best be getting back to Caddie, too."

"See you tomorrow, then?"

"I'm counting on it. Got that outing planned with Mr. Thorn, if you're still up for it."

Walsh nodded wearily. "I'll see y'all there. Be careful overnight, you hear?"

" 'Careful's' my middle name," Finch answered, smiling.

"Guess mine must be 'Handsome,' then," Walsh said.

He started walking back the long way to his own shack in the woods, mulling the subject of their conversation for a while, then letting go of it. When he was halfway there, a twig cracked somewhere in the dark behind him, making Fuller stop and turn around, scanning the night for hidden enemies.

"Somebody there?" he called, expecting no reply and getting none.

Nothing, he thought, before a hard, blunt object smashed into his skull behind one ear and put him down.

TWELVE

OUTSIDE WASHINGTON, MISSISSIPPI: JUNE 23, 1877

Yancy Olson and his whitecaps had transported Fuller Marsh six miles northeast of Natchez, stagger-stumbling behind one of their horses with his wrists bound, hooded, falling twice along the way and being dragged a bit each time, to reach the wooded area they sought.

Washington, another half mile up the road, had been the longest-serving capital of Mississippi Territory, seventeen years before statehood, but it wasn't much to look at now. Named for America's first president, it had a school Jefferson Davis had attended while a boy of ten, but its population had dwindled since then, with most of its present-day population consisting of freedmen.

That was one reason Olson had selected the location for interrogation of his prisoner, two birds, one stone. Besides intimidation of the dusky locals, though, he also reckoned that no one would interrupt his posse at its work.

On arrival, they had stripped Walsh of his clothes and

tied him up securely to a stout loblolly pine, hugging its trunk. Before they started asking any questions, Walsh was given fifteen lashes with a bullwhip, opening his back so that a couple of his ribs were visible through welling blood. They had to splash stream water on him after that, to bring him back around, then Yancy stepped in close and started quizzing him.

At first, Walsh had denied any acquaintance with Erasmus Finch, but they had let him see a fireplace poker heating in an open fire, its tip already glowing red, and he'd admitted they were longtime friends.

That was enough to get him killed right there, but Yancy still wanted to know of their connection to the Bostonian who dressed in black and didn't seem to mind race-mixing. Walsh had balked again at that, until the poker lightly grazed his cheek and plunged him once again into unconsciousness.

"Be careful, dammit!" Yancy snapped at his companions. "This'll take all night if he keeps passing out."

When he came around the second time, his left eye nearly swollen shut, Yancy resumed his questioning but got no further with it than the prisoner's admission of consorting with a former field slave. Finally, with dawn encroaching on their privacy and nothing more to show for so much effort, Olson called a halt to the proceedings, fuming inwardly at yet another failure.

How many more second chances would he get before Chief Hightower decided Yancy was expendable?

The whitecap leader felt as if he were already stomping on thin ice, with fissured spreading out in all directions. He could almost hear their crackling, then snapped out of it and realized that he was hearing logs pop in the fire nearby.

"We're getting nowhere," Olson told his men, as if they hadn't worked that out already for themselves.

Drawing a Colt pocket revolver from his belt, the so-called "Baby Dragoon," Yancy stepped in close and fired a .31-caliber bullet into the base of their prisoner's skull at skin-touch range. Warm blood spattered over his hand and wrist, the smell of burnt hair mingling with the odors of seared flesh and woodsmoke.

Done.

"Untie 'im," he instructed. "Dump 'im near the river but not in it. I want this one found to send a message loud and clear."

He didn't bother saying what that message was supposed to be. The boys could work that out among themselves, if they were so inclined. Call it a warning signal against whites and blacks pretending they were friendly, much less equal to each other, or the interloper down from Massachusetts might decide he'd overstayed his welcome in Natchez.

If nothing else, Chief Hightower would hear of it and realize that he'd been underestimating Olson at his peril. Maybe from this point on, Yancy would get the damned respect he was entitled to.

Or would it blow up in his face, as the fiasco back in Silver Street had done?

He could imagine that occurring, knew that next time he would not survive it. To avoid the terminal displeasure of his masters, Yancy figured that he still had something left to do.

He had to stop the man in black from acting out his plan —whatever that might be—to haul a monster from the Mississippi and mark Natchez as a town accursed.

Somehow, he had to stop the Yankee dead.

NATCHEZ

After a visit to the barn behind the Haverstock Hilltop hotel, Thorn walked to Pepper Jack's for breakfast, musing that he had become a regular without ever intending to.

After last night's ambush, Gideon passed on sitting at his table facing onto Silver Street. There was no point in helping other gunmen pin him down while placing innocent townspeople in the line or fire. Instead, he chose a table in one of the restaurant's rear corners, seated with his back against the wall, with a clear view of anyone who entered after him.

The other breakfast diners, some of whom he recognized for sharing space at other meals, were careful to avoid meeting Thorn's eyes this morning. Those seated at tables nearest to him broke off normal conversation, lapsing into silence save for curt requests to pass the toast, the salt or pepper. Others, farther off, shot sidelong glances toward him while their conversations dropped from normal tones to cautious whispers.

None of that was new or strange to Gideon. When Chief Hightower passed the restaurant, striding along from north to south, Thorn half expected him to enter from the street, renew their argument from last night and create a scene, but if the chief saw him at all, he gave no sign of it.

Thorn ordered two fried eggs with buttermilk pancakes and maple syrup, working through it in his own good time with coffee on the side. He thought about his plan to meet again with Finch and Walsh today, take out the *Sturgeon* for another run, and see what they might fine.

Before they launched, he'd have to brief them on his plan for luring the creature out of hiding, finding some way to explain the scheme that didn't make them think they'd sided with a raving lunatic.

No easy task, but Thorn reckoned he'd find a way.

In fact, if Finch and Walsh were game for hunting monsters underwater, they'd already demonstrated a propensity for taking strange events on faith.

But would his plan succeed, or was he simply wasting everybody's time?

Last night, his second try at reaching out to find the creature, Gideon had rated the attempt successful. Still, he couldn't say how distance, river traffic, even simply sunlight, might affect the outcome of his most important test. If he could not renew his contact with the beast, whatever it might be, would that signal the ending of his hunt, or should he try and try again until another fragile mind link was regained?

Thorn's meal arrived and he dug in, still checking out the street door every time he raised a forkful to his mouth, and at the same time listening for any racket from the kitchen, heralding arrival of attackers through the restaurant's backdoor. None came for him, supporting Thorn's initial verdict that the whitecaps were a gang of cowards who preferred to work their mischief in the dark.

On top of that, counting the three he'd killed last night and one he'd wounded at their first encounter, out on Cottonwood, there was a chance the group was running short of members prone to risking life and limb.

Would they back off and let Thorn work in peace?

He thought the odds supporting that were slim to none.

Bullies might run when met with force, but they were also prone to nursing grudges, coming back around to settle things once they had gained some distance from the object of their fear. In groups, goading each other to repair a battered reputation, they might come around more quickly than if it were only one or two of them acting alone.

The moral of that story: Thorn would have to keep his eyes wide open, hoping he could trust Erasmus Finch and Fuller Walsh to watch his back should they proceed.

And at the same time he would have to find a man-killing anomaly of nature, track it down, and rid the Mississippi River of it if he could.

Leaving the restaurant, his bill settled, together with a tip, Thorn had to ask himself if aiding Dixie, breeding ground of slavery and treason to the Union, was a task worth undertaking in the first place. And he wound up answering that question with a solid "Yes."

Regardless of their other faults, the citizens of Mississippi and Louisiana, black and white alike, deserved to lead their lives without the nagging dread of being snatched and eaten by some unknown predator.

With that in mind, he walked back to the Haverstock Hilltop, fetched Shadow from his stall, and got him saddled for the road.

When Jubal Kenfield went to circulate the *Natchez Independence*'s "Extra" edition, he made sure to take his Colt Sidehammer Model 1855 along with him, hidden beneath his jacket, tucked into his belt around in back so that its butt rubbed up against his spine, its post front sight digging into the cleft between his nether cheeks.

The newsman seriously doubted whether he could draw and fire it fast enough to save himself from harm, but he was bound to try, would not allow masked bullies to control his life.

Kenfield had priced the "Extras" at a nickel each and he

was cleaning up on sales, unloading half of them before he'd even cleared the block of Silver Street where last night's battle had occurred. He calculated that his eyewitness description of the row between Gideon Thorn and Natchez's police chief would provoke a furious reaction from Hal Hightower, but Jubal had his facts straight and his shorthand notes supporting them. If sued for libel, he was ready to assert truth as an absolute defense.

Of course, what others might decide to do about his editorial remained an open question, hence the gun wedged underneath his belt.

The whitecaps were another problem altogether.

While Chief Hightower had sworn an oath to keep the peace—at least by daylight, in the public eye—no such restriction bound the county's nightriders. Kenfield had gathered information on their crimes since Reconstruction's end: at least one lynching, half a dozen acts of arson, random beatings, gunfire, vandalism. So far, he'd refrained from publishing a tabulation of those incidents because he lacked hard evidence to blame a given member of the shrouded brotherhood in print.

That *would* be libel, barring evidence sufficient to support indictment and conviction in a courtroom, and the felons he denounced could wind up owning Jubal's newspaper and home, while he was driven out of Adam's County in disgrace, a pauper.

No.

He had to pick his battles carefully, with some advance prospect of winning, and he had not found the proper ammunition yet.

The time might come, but until then...

"Some action last night, eh?"

The question came from butcher Eddie Green, sweeping

the wooden sidewalk fronting on his shop as Kenfield paused to let him finish.

"Yes, indeed," Jubal replied. "One nickel for full details, as it happened."

"I can do that," Green replied, digging into a pocket of his trousers to retrieve the coin and hand it over. Kenfield was departing, five cents richer, when the butcher stopped him short. "You hear about that fella turned up dead down by the river, earlier today?"

Feeling his stomach lurch, Jubal replied, "Not yet, I haven't. Any idea who it was?"

"A white man's all I heard," Green said. "Sounds like he met somebody in the wrong place at the wrong time."

"I'll look into it, and thanks!" said Kenfield, handing back the butcher's nickel. "My treat, Mr. Green."

Sweating, he scurried off with papers underneath one arm, the ink staining his shirt, to find out whether Thorn was still alive.

"Goddamn it all to Hell!"

Grover Arquette crumpled his copy of the *Natchez Independent* in his fist and flung it at his guest, across the broad plain of his desk. Seated directly opposite, Chief Hightower allowed the wad of newsprint to bounce off his chest and rattle to the office floor between his boots.

"I know it's bad," Hightower said.

"Oh, well, that's hunky-dory, then," Arquette snapped back at him. "As long as *you* know that it's bad, I'm so relieved that I could dance a naked jig around the courthouse. Thanks so goddamn much for taking *that* load off my mind!"

"I didn't mean—"

"Shut up!" the Democratic Party leader raged. "I don't care what you *meant,* for God's sake! Did you say this shit, or not?"

"Well..."

"With that goddamn Jubal Kenfield standing right there, taking notes. You could've gone all out and had Sy Givens fetch his camera. Hell, we could send a photo to the *New York Times* and make sure everybody in the world knows all about it. How'd that be?"

"I didn't say—"

"Did you just hear me tell you to shut up? Or are you deaf, as well as dumb?"

"No, sir." Hightower's face flushed crimson, but he knew when it was safe to speak and when the consequences might be catastrophic for him. "I mean, yes, I heard you."

"But you still keep talking. Why is that?"

Hightower was about to answer, had his mouth open in fact, then saw the trap ahead of him swallowed back whatever he had meant to say.

Arquette shifted directions, asking him, "Were these three stiffs all whitecaps."

"Sir, there's no hard proof of that."

"Give me a simple 'yes' or 'no', Chief."

"I'm saying nobody can prove it, one way or the other."

Arquette rocked back in his desk chair, staring at the chief as if Hightower's face had just sprouted a second nose. "Nobody? What about that bunghole Yancy Olson? Is he still their 'secret' leader, or has that changed overnight?"

"He wouldn't squeal on us," Hightower said.

"First thing," Arquette replied with acid dripping from his voice, "there ain't no *us*. I never told you to do anything about this Boston Yankee, did I? Well, *did* I?"

"No, sir. Nothing."

"No. You're goddamn right I never, so there's no *us* in this deal at all."

Instead of answering that time, Hightower bobbed his head in the affirmative, like a ventriloquist's dummy.

"All right. That's settled, then. Next thing, I need to know right now if *you* said anything to Olson about taking down this—what's his name, again?"

"Gideon Thorn."

"Right. *Did* you, Chief?"

"I didn't tell 'im no such thing, sir."

"But...?"

"But what?"

"Jesus! What *did* you tell him?"

"Well, I might've said we didn't want no further trouble from the Yankee or his lawyers. Could have told him nothing should be *seen* to happen, but if Thorn was just to up and disappear, like—"

"Stop right there! I won't hear any more of this, but you need to keep something clear in mind. You listening to me?"

"Yes, sir."

"If Olson thinks he's going down, who do you think he's gonna point a finger at to keep himself from getting hung?"

Arquette could see Hightower working on it, looking like a man who'd had a piece of rancid pork for supper and was just about to bring it up again.

"Son of a bitch!" Hightower muttered, almost whispering.

"Well, praise the Lord. You see it now?"

"I do, sir."

"You'll agree that Yancy must not be allowed to spill his version of the story?"

"Yes, sir. I can—"

"Hush! We never had this conversation, Chief. If you claim otherwise, I'll swear you're lying. And the judges in this district owe their jobs to me."

"I understand, sir."

"Good. If I was you, I wouldn't waste another second."

"No."

"So, why 'n hell are you still sitting here?"

FOUR MILES NORTHEAST OF NATCHEZ

Erasmus Finch was waiting with his mule when Thorn arrived on Shadow, reining in outside the swaybacked barn that hid the *Sturgeon* and its wagon.

"Still waiting on Walsh?" he asked.

"Fuller ain't coming," Finch replied.

Gideon frowned at that. Asked Finch, "What changed his mind?"

"A bullet," Finch replied. "Somebody found 'im out on Cottonwood a little after sunup. Seems he took a whipping and was burnt a bit before one of the men that grabbed him finished it."

"Whitecaps?"

"If not them, then maybe police. Whoever did it snatched him up after we had a talk last night. He never made it home."

"What's your best guess for how they chose him?"

"Could've followed 'im—or me, for that matter. Didn't want to shoot us outright, maybe hunting information and decided that a white man would know more or give it up quicker."

"That does it for the *Sturgeon* then, I guess," Thorn said.

"Not necessarily."

"It takes three men to operate it, though."

"It takes three if you've got 'em," Finch replied, half smiling. "If you come up short, though, two can run it in a pinch."

"How's that?"

"You have an empty seat amidships, one scoots up to turn the screws and man the rudder, both. Leaves one to use the scope and fire the spar torpedo. I don't say it's *easy*, mind you, but it can be done."

"Meaning the two of us," Thorn clarified.

"Who else we got?"

"That would increase the risk."

"No doubt," Finch said. "But look at it another way. Whoever takes her down is gambling with his life. No promise that three men can bring it back safe, any more than two."

"And two men use less oxygen than three," Thorn mused.

"Don't smell as bad, neither, they start in sweating."

"No," Gideon granted.

"Only leaves one problem to my way of thinking."

"How to find the thing we're looking for?"

"You hit in on the head," said Finch.

"I may have an idea as far as that goes," Thorn replied.

"You wanna share it?"

"It's a stretch. I'm not sure you'd believe me."

"Say again?" This time Finch did smile. "We're about to go in hunting for kind o' monster no one ever saw before, and do it one man short, but now you think I'm turning skeptical?"

"All right, then," Thorn replied. "I'll have to start from the beginning, though."

"Best way I know to tell a story."

Frowning, Gideon began. "When I was three years old..."

THIRTEEN

NATCHEZ

Chief Hightower's fury had not faded since he was dismissed from Grover Arquette's office, rather escalating to the point that he now suffered from a pounding headache and a sour stomach which a double shot of Old Grand-Dad Kentucky bourbon only served to aggravate.

Hightower was fed up with taking Arquette's insults, rolling over like an old dog that was used to being whipped and kicked, but he saw no way out that offered any prospect of relief.

No way aside from beating Arquette to a bloody pulp, at least, and that would mean a trip to prison, where an ex-police chief's life expectancy was nil.

One thing he *could* do was to pass the fury on to someone under his immediate control, and Arquette's snotty lecture had already put a target squarely in his sights.

Yancy Olson had botched the relatively simple job Hightower had assigned to him, ridding Natchez of one unwelcome Yankee, and had bungled it so badly—twice, in fact—that now Grover Arquette was howling for his scalp. That was the kind of cleanup chore Hightower had performed on several occasions, but now Yancy had dropped out of sight as if he knew his head was on the chopping block.

Hightower had already checked two dives where Olson spent much of his time aside from night-riding, cadging free drinks with an implied threat that the whitecaps might come calling if their leader was not amply lubricated. Somehow, Yancy had never figured out that anyone who threw his weight around too much might end his days as gator bait.

But Hightower still had to find him first.

It was a disadvantage, searching on his own with no help from his officers, but this was one job that Hightower had to do alone. If he had mobilized his men to search for Olson, questions would be raised when Olson disappeared —and more so if he turned up dead.

In that case, Chief Hightower knew he couldn't count on any help from Arquette or the crooked pawns he had installed in public office since the war. In fact, Arquette would mobilize the Adams County justice system to get rid of Hightower if necessary, making sure the chief could never point a finger at him from a witness stand.

Not that a jury anywhere in Mississippi would convict Arquette of anything.

They might believe that he was guilty, but that didn't count for much in the Magnolia State. Conviction would bring ruin down upon the jurors who saw fit to buck the system and whoever was the governor when Arquette got around to sentencing would likely grant a pardon in return for favors owed.

No, Hightower thought, deciding that he just might need another shot or three of booze to ease the pain inside his skull. The only way he could protect himself was by obeying orders, getting rid of Olson before Yancy made things any worse.

But who to ask?

The answer hit him like a slap across the face, Hightower grimacing at his own mental sluggishness for taking so long to divine it.

Other whitecaps were most likely to have some idea of where their leader was, Hightower could squeeze them till they squealed, the old carrot and stick approach to problem-solving. He could offer promotion of a useful tattletale to Yancy's spot as leader of the nightriders. Then, if the information helped locate his man, the chief could always change his mind, dealing with Olson *and* the guy who'd sold him out.

What sort of fool would take his word as gospel on a deal like that?

The kind who pulled a flour sack over his head at night and rode around inflicting misery on those who didn't dare fight back. The same cretin who might imagine that he had the chief over a barrel and could make demands for special favors somewhere down the line.

Good luck with that.

If there was one thing Hal Hightower absolutely knew first-hand, it was the value of a finely executed double-cross.

NORTH OF NATCHEZ

Launching the *Sturgeon*, one man short, turned out to be as difficult as Gideon expected, but there was no option of enlisting anybody else to help them out. He and Erasmus Finch would do it on their own or it would not get done.

The good news was that Finch had readily accepted Thorn's account of how he'd learned to share his thoughts with certain animals without resort to spoken words. In fact, the freedman seemed to take it all in stride, stating the obvious—that animals without the gift of speech were not equipped to translate English anyhow, but still seemed to communicate among themselves with no great difficulty.

"Caddie's mama had the second sight," Finch had explained. "And some years back, during the war, I ran across a colored fella from Louisiana, called himself a *houngan*. You know what that means?"

"One name for a Voodoo priest," Thorn answered.

"That's it in a nutshell," Finch confirmed.

In fact, from reading Aunt Drusilla's books on occult matters, Gideon had been conversant with the rules and language of Voodoo—derived from *Vodun*, brought halfway around the world by kidnapped Africans, then mixed into a heady stew with bits of Christianity—before he had endured his close encounter with the sect three months ago, in Arkansas.

That case had put him up against a ruthless *hougan* and his female counterpart, a *mambo* in cult jargon who were bent on using zombies—said to be reanimated corpses—to their personal advantage. Dinah Pilcher had come along with Thorn for that excursion into darkness and had nearly lost her life as a result. Beyond that, it was touch-and-go recovering her fragile sanity, but if Obi Magoro's telegrams were accurate, Dinah was on her way to something like a full recovery.

Gideon kept that information to himself, and Finch was not the sort of man to pry unnecessarily.

Besides, they had their hands full as it was, hauling *Sturgeon* to the same point where they'd launched it yesterday and making final preparations for the hunt to come.

Besides the submarine, they took along one of its spar torpedoes, waiting till they'd reached the Mississippi where they'd carried out their first test run. Erasmus knew how to attach it to the *Sturgeon*'s prow but warned against it until they had reached the sheltered cove and verified that no one else was lurking in the woods nearby.

Before that, Finch opened the *Sturgeon*'s access hatch and climbed inside, emerging only when he'd changed the submarine's seating for three, permitting Finch to serve dual functions as the boat's animate engine and controller of its rudder.

Thorn crawled in when Finch was finished with the overhaul, taking the seat once occupied by Fuller Walsh, confirming the he understood the boat's "polemoscope" viewing device and could control it. At the same time, he observed cable that protruded through the boat's hull, lying near the captain's seat, a wooden handle at that end permitting Gideon to tug the line and trigger the torpedo's war head once he got it planted in the target of his choice.

If he could call the creature into striking range. If it had not swum off to parts unknown. And if it didn't wreck the *Sturgeon* first, leaving its crew to drown while mired in Mississippi River mud.

Too many *ifs*, but there no alternative approach came to his mind.

Back in fresh air and sunlight, Gideon helped Finch attach the spar torpedo and secure its trigger line. The wooden shaft's butt end was capped with metal, threaded like a screw, which fit inside a corresponding pocket on the

Sturgeon's tapered bow. The trigger cable passed from inside the submersible through a small hole caulked with oakum, overlaid with axle grease to ward off catastrophic leakage.

At the loose end of that cable was a metal clip that Gideon attached to a small loop at the end of the spar torpedo's trigger line. That done, a sharp tug from his seat inside the *Sturgeon* would drop a percussion hammer onto the explosive's fuse and spark a chain-reaction in the manner of a flintlock firearm.

That could be another thing that foiled their scheme. The fuse might be too old to function properly, although his eyes found no corrosion present. They could not test the torpedo in advance, fearing its explosion might draw witnesses, and if the first charge blew as ordered, that still would not prove the sole remaining weapon would perform on cue.

Conversely, if the charge was planted in their living target but refused to detonate for any reason, it would leave the *Sturgeon*'s two-man crew unarmed and hopeless.

Still, it was their only chance.

Finished preparing for a climax that might never come, Thorn rose and turned to Finch.

"All set," he said. "You ready?"

"As I'll ever be," Erasmus Finch replied.

"Looking for me, you say?"

"Way I heard it," Gavin Grisby said, and spat tobacco juice into the forge that kept his blacksmith's shop feeling like summer all year round.

"What for?" asked Yancy Olson.

Grisby shrugged. "Don't know, but he was in with

Grover and the word is Hal came out looking like someone pissed on 'im and told 'im it was raining."

"Damn."

The only "Grover" Olson knew or ever heard of was the district's Democratic Party boss, and he could only have a mad on against Yancy for one reason that came readily to mind.

Gideon Thorn.

If Hightower was tracking him on orders from Arquette, it likely meant the big man had decided to get rid of Yancy based on the attempts Olson had bungled, first trying to run the Yankee out of town, and then to silence him for good.

Since he'd received that order from the chief, four men were dead and two of Olson's whitecaps were at home licking their wounds. It took no great imagination to work out that Arquette's next move would be getting rid of Olson, though he'd never do the dirty work himself.

That's what police were for in Mississippi.

Maybe reading worry on his captain's face, Grisby asked Olson, "What you gonna do?"

Thc first answer that came to mind was getting out of town and out of Adams County, but Yancy was kissing-close to broke and frankly couldn't think of any place to go. Nowhere that Arquette couldn't find him, anyhow.

"I need to make this right," he said, thinking aloud, having no reason to believe Grisby could help him out."

Still, he was bound to try.

"One thing I've learnt," the whitecap blacksmith said, "is that when folks is mad at you, they'll calm down if you do a favor for 'em."

Great, thought Yancy. *Now I get advice from this dumb peckerwood who barely learnt to write his name.*

Still, he had to ask. "What kind of favor would that be, exactly?"

"Maybe catch that Boston Yankee meddling where he don't belong and using war materials to do it."

Baffled, Yancy challenged, "What in hell does that mean, Gavin?"

"You don't know about the submarine?"

"*What* submarine?"

"The one that Fuller Walsh made off with after Appomattox. Rumor has it that he's got it stashed somewhere outside of town."

Olson felt hot blood rushing to his face, burning his cheeks from the inside. A feeble ray of hope lanced through the darkness in his head.

"Gavin," he said, "go back and start from the beginning now, and don't leave nothing out."

MIDSTREAM, OFFSHORE FROM NATCHEZ

The creature felt another tug inside its skull, stronger than either time before. It shuddered for an instant, not from any chill the great river imparted through its hide or layers of body fat, but more akin to an electric current passing through the water from a distant lightning strike.

It still could not decipher if the source of that niggling disturbance to its brain and nervous system emanated from a food or from potential food. Indeed, the swimmer did not know it *had* a brain, much less a web of nerves extending from its snout along the full length of body, twenty yards or more, down to the relatively small fluke at its tail's end.

Its first instinct was to escape, reverse directions and thrash on downstream until it put enough distance between itself and its tormenter to escape the feeling that its skull had been invaded, occupied and turned against its will.

But just as quickly as that fragmentary thought took shape, the beast rejected it. It was accustomed to its role, being the largest predator within its range, on land or in the water. In its time, the creature had devoured swimming reptiles of all sizes, birds that settled on the river's surface, and on mammals of all sizes, ranging from otters and beavers, livestock, once a cougar lapping water, and of late the upright apes who clothed themselves in tasteless fabric, bent on souring the pleasure of an easy meal.

The beast was not afraid per se but wanted to identify the irritant that had assailed it three times now, within a single cycle of the sun and moon above. That entity—a living thing; the beast felt sure of that—was drawing closer now, if only slowly, followed by a grinding, churning sound the predator could not identify.

No skittish ungulate that fled from danger on dry land, no timid fish that joined a school for safety's sake but still lived constantly in fear, the predator put more strength behind the movements of its supple tail, propelling it on a collision course toward impact with the object that perplexed it so.

Whatever sought it, even tried to summon it, was in for a surprise.

The adversary did not know what it was doing, calling down a storm with no idea of consequences. It had obviously never seen the predator before, had never watched it feed.

It was about to learn the gravity of its mistake, and that would be the final lesson of its wasted life.

A forty-five-ton juggernaut was bearing down upon it swiftly, almost silently, without a hint of warning.

And the juggernaut had teeth.

Even with Fuller Walsh removed, the *Sturgeon*'s twenty-odd foot cabin still felt humid and musty. Thorn had removed his hat to keep its brim from butting up against the eyepiece of the small submersible's polemoscope and as last time, he was perspiring freely in the confines of its stuffy atmosphere.

During the war, another Rebel sub, the *H. L. Hunley*, had been ten feet longer than the *Sturgeon*, sailing with one officer and seven other men on board. He wondered how the crew had managed, then remembered that they hadn't. Five were killed in the *Hunley*'s first test run, and all eight on her second. Finally, before its first engagement with a Union warship, the Confederacy had recruited two Germans, one Dane and one Brit to sign on for an attack against the sloop-of-war USS *Housatonic.* A torpedo sank the *Housatonic*, but its blast had also breached the *Hunley*'s hull, claiming the lives of all aboard.

All told, the Rebs lost twenty-one men and their submersible against a score of five U.S. fatalities.

Thorn hoped his voyage in the *Sturgeon* wouldn't be a replay of the not-so-distant past.

Seated behind him, Finch was breathing heavily from his exertion on the screws and rudder, both hands occupied while Gideon instructed him on where to go, which way to turn and when. There were onions on his breath, which made the pent-up air inside the submarine smell stronger than their last time out.

That time had only been a test run. Now that they were hunting actively, Thorn couldn't say how much time might elapse before they let it go and started back to shore.

Eyeing the Mississippi's surface through his scope, tracking for any vessels that might pose a danger to the *Sturgeon*, Thorn had no vie of the river's murky depths. Unable to employ his eyes, he beamed his thoughts out through the submarine's metallic hull and off along the river's current, seeking a response.

Ten minutes passed, and then fifteen. Gideon reckoned they were coming up on twenty when a pulse behind his left eye signaled contact.

But with what?

He had been able to commune with snakes before, including one time when a rattler crept into his bedroll and Thorn woke to find the serpent coiled upon his chest, warming itself. On that occasion he had sent the would-be killer packing, tiny mind in disarray, but he had never tried it on a crocodilian and had no idea what sort of message would rebound to him if one of them replied.

This mental "touch" was unlike anything that Gideon had ever felt before. He could not peg it as to species, couldn't even say if it was mammal, reptile, or something entirely different. He *did* gain an impression of stupendous size and weight, although attempts to forge a mental image of the thing defeated him.

He only knew that it was huge, heavy, and heading on a hard collision course to the *Sturgeon*.

Gideon turned back from the scope and told Finch, "We've got something headed this way. Something big."

"What kind of something?" asked Erasmus.

"I can't answer that," Thorn said, "but we should hang on tight. It's in a rotten mood."

"I'm starting to regret this," Finch replied. "Feels like it might just be the worst idea I ever hatched."

"We're in it now," said Gideon. "Too late for us to turn around."

"How far off do you make it?"

"That's a problem," Thorn admitted. "Closer than it was, but I don't know for sure. It could be anywhere from—"

At that instant, a titanic weight collided with the *Sturgeon,* nearly rolled it over to Thorn's right, then raised the submarine as something long and sleek swept past beneath their keel.

"Sweet Jesus!" Finch cried out, then muttered, "Sorry, Lord."

Gideon wasn't sure if what he felt next was a swirling in the river's current or within his mind. Whichever, he was not inclined to credit nature for the sudden chill he felt.

"Hang on!" he cautioned Finch. "It's coming back for more."

FOURTEEN

NATCHEZ WATERFRONT

"Hurry up, dammit! We're wasting time!"

A dozen sullen-looking whitecaps glared at Yancy Olson while they trooped aboard two steamboats, commandeered from skippers overawed by Olson's reputation, bluster and the guns his men were brandishing. One was the *Triton,* forty-odd feet long. The other, slightly smaller, had been christened *Sprite.* Both normally ran ferry service back and forth between Vidalia and Natchez, but they would transport no more paying customers today.

Yancy was last to board the *Triton,* carrying a double-barreled shotgun, with a pistol wedged under his belt because he didn't own a holster. All the other raiders had at least one firearm each, most of them double that, but they were clearly skittish about setting off on stolen vessels to pursue a wartime submarine and the elusive, possibly imaginary creature it was hunting.

One problem, to Yancy's certain knowledge, was that roughly half his whitecaps couldn't swim and some of those who *could* were no great shakes at it, some of them barely able to sustain a dogpaddle. Outsiders might have been surprised that anybody born and raised along the Mississippi had not learned to swim, but with the yearly rate of local drownings, many youngsters were discouraged by their parents from approaching the great river, much less diving in.

The second problem weighing Yancy's shoulders down today was Chief Hightower and his cops. Most Natchez officers felt friendly toward the whitecaps—some of them were even not-so-secret members—but the chief was out for Olson's scalp and Yancy stealing two boats gave Hightower ample cause to run him in.

And once Olson was locked away in jail, there was no telling what might happen next, including a staged "accident" that might prove fatal with no blame accruing to the chief.

Screw that, he thought. If Yancy's stars aligned to make this day his last, he planned on doing one last thing to cinch his reputation as a man who went all out to help the Anglo-Saxon race.

In truth, he didn't have a clue who Anglo-Saxons were, or had been, other than the fact that they were white—and what else really mattered in the South?

The *Triton*'s steam engine rumbled to life belowdecks, its vibrations traveling through Olson's boot soles, up his legs and spreading to his innards. He regretted the decision to go fishing for Navy-surplus submarine but couldn't turn back now.

Better to die out on the open water than to be regarded as a coward and a fool.

His biggest problem now, aside from stealing boats worth more than Yancy earned in any given five-year stretch, was total ignorance of where Erasmus Finch and Fuller Walsh had stashed the *Sturgeon* after Appomattox, when surrender brought an end to war except for certain die-hard Rebels like the James and Younger boys.

Just now, Yancy wished he was far away from Natchez, riding with those boys and living high off loot they stole from banks and trains.

Another dream derailed.

Olson's last-minute plan, hardly deserving of that term, involved his whitecaps searching up and down the shoreline till the *Sturgeon* showed itself, then chasing after it and sinking it for good, with Finch and Thorn aboard. Now that he thought about it, Yancy wasn't sure the guns they'd brought along would even pierce the *Sturgeon*'s cast-iron hull, but like so much else in his life, it was too late to turn back now.

At least he'd managed to secure the boats and put his men on board. They were proceeding north, upstream against the Mississippi's current, where they'd either find the submarine or they would not.

In either case, thought Olson, this would likely be his last day as a free white man.

MIDSTREAM, NORTH OF NATCHEZ

Inside the *Sturgeon*, iron rings had been welded to its bulkhead, handholds that vaguely resembled rungs of a long ladder lying on its side. Before their prey collided with the submarine, Gideon grabbed one of those rings to brace himself and leaned back from eyepiece of the *Sturgeon*'s polemoscope.

That backwards movement saved him from a forehead gash or worse as something large and heavy crashed into the submarine a second time. Glancing around, he saw Erasmus Finch seated in profile, cranking the propellers' crooked handle with his right hand, tugging on the rudder's upright lever with his left. Thorn caught a glimpse of desperation in the freedman's eyes, but also saw excitement mirrored there.

"You figured out what that thing is yet?" Finch inquired.

"Still haven't seen it," Gideon replied. "It has to break the surface before I can spot it through the scope."

"Seems like it's got another plan," Finch said. "Like sinking us."

Thorn knew he should have banked on that, but how would it have made a difference? He had to work within the limits of the submarine's design. There were no underwater windows, since they might be smashed and flood the boat's interior. As far as catching sight of their attacker through the scope, he knew that it would only surface if it was an air-breather, meaning a mammal or a reptile. And in that case, the odds against Thorn making a split-second sighting would be astronomical.

This, he concluded, was a fight they must conduct as if it were a game of blind man's bluff, the loser marked for death.

Without seeing their enemy, Thorn could not judge its size or shape, could not determine any weak points it might have. Worse yet, the thing was free to charge and batter them from any side, while Gideon could only use the *Sturgeon*'s spar torpedo if they rammed the beast head-on. And even that might prove fruitless, depending on the predator's morphology, the shape and thickness of its skull, together with a hide that might be armored like a crocodile's.

Still, Thorn could only play the hand he had been dealt and try to do it blindfolded.

One law of nature was that every living thing must take in nourishment. Apart from certain small invertebrates who "drank" a portion of their nutrients through moist and porous skin, that meant the river beast must have a mouth, presumably located at the forepart of its head or face. If, like most swimming creatures, it possessed no grasping limbs—and nothing of the kind had been employed against the submarine so far—said mouth would likely open during an attack, to either damage an opponent or consume intended prey.

And if the creature's mouth was open when it charged the *Sturgeon*...

From behind him, Finch spoke up, saying, "I hope you got a bright idea to get us outa this."

"I might," Thorn said. "But there's a risk attached."

"No shit? More risk than being sunk and drowned?"

"We could be blown to smithereens," Gideon said.

"At least that's quick. I'd rather go that way than being gobbled up alive."

"Okay, then," Thorn replied. "I'll see what I can do."

"Just do it quick, will you? I've got some seepage building up back here. Another hit or two like the last one, this tub is gonna fill up pretty quick."

Gideon turned his mind back toward the creature he had lured from the Mississippi's depths, seeking contact and finding it with the familiar sense of churning in his brain. As best he could, Thorn flashed an image of the *Sturgeon* to the monster bent on killing him, imagined it charging the submarine head-on with jaws agape, ready to maul or swallow it.

The answer he got back in turn was movement, an

immense form rushing through the water, tail thrashing to help it pick up speed. It seemed to be approaching from his left-front, midway between the numbers ten and eleven on an imaginary clock's face. If it held that course, it would collide with Finch's submarine at an angle of thirty degrees, give or take a fraction.

That meant missing the spar torpedo's lethal charge and maybe snapping off its wooden shaft if the attacker followed through by snapping at the *Sturgeon*'s prow. In that case, they would be disarmed, with no recourse except to flee at top speed from a beast that had already proved itself larger and faster than the submarine.

"Turn left!" he called to Finch.

"How far?"

"Picture a pocket watch. Try eleven o'clock."

"Starting now!" Finch called back, nearly shouting despite the short distance between them.

"Ramming speed!" Thorn answered back. "And brace yourself!"

Chief Hightower and five patrolmen were aboard the ferry *Madeleine*, northbound in hot pursuit of Yancy Olson's stolen boats.

The chief had left his fifteen other day-shift officers in town, patrolling on their normal rounds, while he attempted to regain control of the disturbance that now threated his career, perhaps his very life itself.

Each cop riding the *Madeleine* was armed with a Winchester "Yellow Boy," the model 1866 rifle nicknamed for its receiver molded from a brass/bronze alloy christened "gunmetal." Each lever-action weapon had fifteen .44-40

Winchester rounds in its tubular magazine, plus one in the chamber, and the officers also wore pistols on their hips.

Although outnumbered by the gunmen they were chasing, Hightower believed his people had a fighting chance against Olson's whitecaps. Based on his knowledge of the group, Hightower would have bet that nearly half of them were drunk right now, the rest wishing they were.

And facing well-armed men in uniform was not the same as raiding colored shacks at midnight, shooting frightened farmhands barely roused from sleep.

Hightower's job was twofold as he saw it. First and foremost, Yancy Olson must be silenced for the good of everyone who stood above him in the racist pyramid of Adams County politics and what passed for polite society in Mississippi. Olson living could tell tales that would wreak havoc around Natchez and environs, nattering about the orders he'd been given and had carried out, including homicides. In that regard he literally knew where the bodies were buried and wouldn't be shy about tattling if facing the gallows himself.

Olson stealing the two ferries gave Hightower a sound excuse for killing him and claiming he was shot while threatening police with injury or death. If any of his men were taken in alive, Hightower reckoned one or more could link Yancy to Fuller Walsh's recent murder—gunning down a fellow white man—and that crime along would wipe out any sympathy misguided residents of Natchez might be harboring.

With Yancy dead and gone, Hightower could control the narrative, add any elements that pleased him and omit those that he deemed superfluous or contradictory. Grover Arquette would thus be mollified, his mind at ease, and there would be no cause for him to crucify Hightower or replace him as chief of police.

The best possible outcome that Hightower could imagine featured Olson killing off Gideon Thorn, then being slain himself by duly sworn Natchez police. That way, Thorn's lawyers back in Boston would have no one left to sue for damages and Arquette wouldn't need to exile Chief Hightower.

All that would remain, then, was the river monster, if the damned thing ever had existed in the first place. Given ample time and a cessation of reports, that fear would fade away and turn into another one of countless ghost stories repeated by poor people, white and black, when they were pulling corks on Friday nights.

"I see 'em, Chief!" one of Hightower's officers called out. His name was Vincent Flynn, handing a telescope to Hightower and pointing upstream with his Winchester.

Hightower took the spyglass, focused it, and saw the stolen ferries running side-by-side, accelerating as if focused on a target just around a river bend one mile ahead, invisible to Hightower from where he stood on deck,

"All right!" he shouted to his men in uniform. "Be ready when we pull up into range. Rapping his knuckles sharply on a window of the *Madeleine*'s wheelhouse, Hightower shouted to the ferry's captain, "Pour it on! You let those two boats get away, you'll spend the next year breaking rocks."

The predator has never seen another animal quite like the black antagonist floating before its eyes, so casual and indolent, its speed no match for any other sea- or river-dwelling denizen.

In profile it looks something like a paddlefish, though more than twice the length of normal specimens, and its rostrum is considerably longer and not so much flattened at its tip as sharpened to a point. In that regard, it seems more like a swordfish or a marlin found at sea, though double either's length at full maturity, its forward-pointing bill longer and stouter, without fragile grace. The ridge along its back reminds the creature of a marlin's dorsal fin—although, again, the predator has no words to describe those other species it has cheerfully dismembered and devoured in days past.

After two grating passes at its enemy, the creature realizes that the black creature *feels* wrong, as well as looking out of place. The billed fish that it hunts are softer, sleek and slippery, whereas the thing confronting it today is rough-textured and stiff, no yield of flesh, muscles or spine and ribs within to indicate a lethal striking point. At the same time, the hunter knows its prey cannot be one of the sea turtles it has taken on occasion, clothed in shells of bone or leather with the soft parts wedged inside.

There is, however, *something* squeezed inside the barrel body of its foe.

Something responsible for reaching out invisibly to rake imaginary claws across the monster's brain, delivering a challenge that the predator cannot refuse.

It has no ego but survives on base emotions: hunger, rage and curiosity, together with a swiftly fading urge to procreate that hardly ever troubles it these days. At some subconscious level, it can recognize a challenge and decides it should accept instead of backing down because the river has been good for it, a more than ample source of food.

And having rushed its adversary twice without

inflicting any damage that its eyes and nostrils can detect, it needs to understand this thing.

If it appears to be a long survivor of some dying race, eliminating it will make the river safe again. If more like it are lurking in the Mississippi, and if they prefer to hunt in packs, the predator should leave while it is able, seeking out another cornucopia along the Orinoco or the Amazon.

More names that it will never know or understand.

For now, it is enough to find one enemy drifting before it, issuing a silent challenge to engage in battle to the death.

When that was done, once it had tasted its opponent's vital organs, then it could begin to hunt in peace again.

"It's gaining on us," Gideon warned Finch. "Hold steady as she goes."

"How long?" Finch asked.

"I can't tell that, but closing fast," Thorn said. "I need to hit it with the spar head-on."

"Can't promise I'll hit something neither one of us can see."

"Just do your best," said Gideon. "If we hold on this course—"

When Thorn lost the mind link without a hint of warning, it reminded him of an elastic band snapping inside his head. A sharp pain raced between his temples, then evaporated in the space of a split-second, leaving a faint sense of nausea behind.

"What is it?" Finch demanded from behind him.

"What is *what*?" Thorn answered back.

"Just then, you gave a jerk like someone stuck a hatpin in your backside."

Blinking rapidly to clear his vision, Gideon leaned forward, toward the eyepiece of the submarine's polemoscope. "Something broke the connection," he replied. "It's turned away from us."

"How come?"

"Hang on a minute." Peering through the scope, Thorn saw two steamboats bearing down upon the *Sturgeon*, with a third chasing the forward pair. Armed men were ranged across the width of all three upper decks, one of them in the nearest of the three crafts pointing toward the water's surface, mouthing words inaudible to Thorn.

"Company's coming," he told Finch, briefly describing the tableau spread out before him.

"Any uniforms aboard?" Finch asked.

"The third boat back looks like police," said Gideon. "The other crews aren't wearing badges."

"Masks?" Finch asked. "They look like whitecaps from the other night?"

"They must have left the flour sacks at home," said Gideon.

Just as he spoke, one of the riflemen aboard the nearest ferry aimed his weapon toward the river's surface twenty-five to thirty yards ahead of him and fired. Thorn saw the marksman's bullet splash into the Mississippi, falling well short of the spot where he and Finch now sat becalmed.

More gunmen from the leading boats were firing now, long guns and pistols raising smoke above their ferries' decks. Faint echoes of the fusillade were barely audible inside the *Sturgeon*'s cabin.

"What 'n hell is that?" asked Finch.

"They're' shooting up the river," Gideon replied. "I can't see what they're shooting at, but—"

Then he could, spotting a dark shape as it reared up from the water like a whale breaching at sea. Some of the plainclothes gunmen on the forward ferries dropped their weapons, others firing at the beast that towered over them before its bulk came crashing down.

FIFTEEN

"There it is! You see that damn thing sticking up?"

"Where at?" the whitecap to his left, dull-witted Davey Vinton, head still bandaged from the graze he'd suffered on the night before last.

"There!" repeated Yancy Olson, pointing with his free left hand, his right clutching the Henry rifle he had confiscated from a black man's isolated cabin nine months earlier, after they beat the owner to within a half-inch of his life.

"I don't see nothing," Davey came back at him.

"Use your eyes, for Lord's sake. *There*! Ain't that part of a submarine they hoist above the water when they're prowling?"

"You mean that tube they look through that I read about?"

That was a lie, of course. Davey could no more read than he could fly around the moon.

"Yeah, that," Yancy confirmed. "Right there in front of you!"

"I guess—"

But then they both lost sight of whatever it was, some fifty, sixty feet in front of the *Triton*, as something else, godawful big surfaced between their stolen ferry and the unknown object Olson's eyes had spotted. This was something big—make that gigantic—and it kept on rising up in front of them like it would never stop, bearing a massive head some six feet long with jaws agape.

"The hell is *that*?" screeched Davey, leveling his scattergun and letting go both barrels before Olson could attempt to answer him.

Not that he had an answer or could think of one if he'd been home and dry, with nothing to disturb him as he pondered it all day. It was a monster from nightmare Yancy never had experienced in fact, the worst thing he had ever seen, and that included blood-soaked battlefields during the war when it was difficult, sometimes impossible, to separate the dying from the dead.

Somewhere behind him, someone on the *Sprite* was calling out, "Police! They's coming after us!" but Yancy lost that when the massive beast in front of him let out a roar that sounded like all of the lions over there in darkest Africa combined into a howling choir.

The racket stunned Yancy and sent him tumbling backward to the *Triton*'s deck, losing his rifle and not caring anymore. The Henry would have done no good against this monster, no more than a kid's slingshot with gravel used for ammunition. Olson realized that he was staring down the creature's gullet and he might be sliding down that wet pink shaft in just a few more seconds as the beast bore down on him.

Somebody screamed with Yancy's voice, the panic welling up inside him as he fumbled for his six-gun, lost it from his quaking hand and heard it slide beyond his reach across the *Triton*'s deck.

A heartbeat later, the vast creature hurled itself against the ferry Yancy had purloined at gunpoint from its rightful owner, flipped the vessel up and over like a see-saw with a really fat kid plumping down on one end, rising up into the air while streaming water from its hull, capsizing as it crashed back down and dumped its passengers into the Mississippi's depths.

Sinking, choking, Olson had time to wonder if he might be better off drowning than being eaten, but then his survival instinct took control and sent him thrashing toward the surface, wishing that he knew exactly where in hell that was.

"What's happening up there?" Erasmus Finch demanded, barely choking out the words.

"It's ripping through the boats like they were kindling," Thorn replied, watching the brutal action through their submarine's polemoscope, his brain still having difficulty processing the scene.

"At least that gets the whitecaps off our backs," Finch said, "and welcome to 'em."

"Not just whitecaps," Thorn advised him. "There goes the police boat, too."

The officers on board the third vessel—one of them either Chief Hightower or his twin—had time to see the beast take out two ferry loads of gunmen as if they were nothing, maybe ants riding a leaf across the river's surface, and the sight had shattered their collective nerve. Thorn saw the uniformed patrolmen leaping clear as the titanic predator raced toward them, furrowing the Mississippi with a tall wake creaming up on either side of it.

He'd seen enough to guess what it might be, comparing grim reality with fossils that he'd once seen in a French museum. Unearthed for the first time in the 1830s, christened *Zeuglodon* in the erroneous belief that it might be an ancient reptile, it was now considered one of several prehistoric, predatory whales, yet bore the scientific name *Basilosaurus*, translated from the Greek as "king lizard."

One problem, by whatever name the thing was called: paleontologists agreed that it had gone extinct during the Eocene Epoch, the final specimens wiped out by something no one could agree upon, thirty-three million years ago.

Of course, that wouldn't be the first time scientists were wrong about such things, and Gideon supposed it would not the last.

"What are we gonna do?" Finch asked him, sitting idle for the moment, trusting in the *Sturgeon*'s buoyancy to keep their craft afloat.

"I only see two choices," Thorn replied. "One is to charge in there and try to stick it with the spar torpedo's hook before it turns on us and sends us to the bottom."

"I ain't loving that one," Finch advised him. "What's the other?"

"I can try what I was working on before the whitecaps and police showed up," Gideon said.

"Meaning to call it back on us."

"Unless you have a better plan."

"How 'bout we make for shore and hope nobody notices, especially that thing?"

"You want to settle for your cousin, right?" asked Thorn. "For all the others this thing has been killing and the ones it will from now on if it gets away?"

"I never meant to be a human sacrifice," Finch said.

"Nor me," said Gideon. "But with a bit of luck, I still think we can pull it off."

"You're feeling lucky, are you?"

"Every day I wake up breathing."

"And you're hoping that includes tomorrow?"

Thorn could only smile at that. "Living is hoping," he replied. "If not, why bother?"

"Don't go preachy on me now," Finch answered back. "It doesn't suit you."

"So, you in or out?"

Finch took a moment to respond, then sighed. Said, "What the hell. I'm in."

Chief Halbert Hightower imagined he was caught up in a nightmare, then he hit the water as the ferry *Madeleine* capsized and hurled him overboard. The shock of impact with cold water, sinking in it, choking on it, cleared his head but only made the waking nightmare real.

Hightower had no clue regarding what the river monster was or where it came from, but he was long past denying its existence. Call the thing a dinosaur or Mother Goose for all he cared. He'd seen it, heard its roaring, watched it smash two riverboats and flip his own craft over like a child's toy, and the chief knew that he either had to get away from it or else die trying.

If he made it, reached the Mississippi's shore a hundred yards due west of where he bobbed in sour-tasting water like a fishing float, Hightower thought he just might take off running without any goal in mind, until his strength ran out and he collapsed.

But getting out came first, the odds against that running slim to none.

Hightower had not held onto his rifle when he splashed into the river, and the pistol in his holster, underwater now, was useless to him, simply dead weight bent on drowning him. Even if he could draw and fire the six-gun, it would be like spitting at one of the great African jungle giants, say an elephant or a rhinoceros, before they ground you into bloody pulp.

Since surfacing, he had already seen the beast devour one poor bastard, one of Yancy Olson's whitecaps, who had screamed as he was swallowed, shrill cries smothered as he vanished down the monster's throat.

He'd once observed a kingsnake swallowing a mouse a half inch at a time, but that was nothing. This beast's jaws could snap a man in two or take him down headfirst, whichever method proved the most convenient. And there was no way that a struggling, shrieking victim could prevent it.

Maybe a determined and heroic man, if he was carrying a scythe or had explosives wrapped around his body, could have slain the monster from within, but Hightower had never been a hero nor aspired to any acts of derring-do. Of course, he'd thrown his weight around with lesser men, especially with blacks Hightower didn't even see as being human, but where honest-to-God *heroism* was concerned, he'd obviously missed the boat.

And now the chief was wishing that he'd missed the *Madeleine* as well.

He could have been on shore and dry, instead of being half drowned in the Mississippi, trying to remember any of his long-forgotten childhood prayers.

To Hell with all of that. The Lord supposedly helped those who helped themselves.

In desperation, Chief Hightower struck off toward the river's western shoreline. He was no great swimmer, but still better than other men he saw thrashing helplessly around him, some already going down for the proverbial third time.

And would he stop to help some of them who had come out unprepared to take a dip?

Forget about that pipedream.

In the water, with a monster gulping people down like peanuts, it was each man for himself and let the Devil take the hindmost.

Four long strokes toward shore, then five—when suddenly a bulky shape hove up from somewhere underneath him, butting against Halbert's chin so that his teeth clacked audibly together.

Hightower thought he might have wet himself from fear at that but couldn't rightly say since he was sopping wet from head to toe. Recoiling from the impact with his fists clenched, ready to defend himself, Hightower blinked to clear his eyes and recognized the man who had collided with him.

"You!" he rasped, in an accusatory tone. "What are you doing here?"

In front of Hightower, struggling to keep his bloodied head and face above the river's surface, Yancy Olson answered, "Trying like a bastard not to drown!"

Inflamed by rage, the creature lashed out at the small armada of its mouse-sized enemies, sounding and breaching in their midst to crush their boats and bodies, then resurfacing to do it all again.

The tattered remnants of a man were stuck between its jagged cheek teeth till the creature had briefly submerged and rinsed the bloody pieces from its mouth. Food wasted, but with so much floating all around it, that was no concern.

It was not killing out of hunger, but from anger at the interruption of its battle with the enemy that reached inside its mind. If parts of this or that once living body rippled down its gullet, it did not regurgitate them, but it took no pleasure from the unexpected feast.

Its flesh, above an insulating layer of blubber, stung from pinpricks that its small and fragile adversaries had inflicted, each accompanied by noise apparently designed to mimic thunderclaps. Were those the sounds it had been hearing from the shore these past two nights? Had its peculiar, awkward enemies been stinging one another or some lesser beings in the darkness when those echoes reached the creature's ears?

No matter.

Wallowing, the predator rolled over on the river's turgid surface once, twice, three times in succession. It lashed out with its forelimbs, slippers nearly four feet long, fracturing skulls and vertebrae, disjointing limbs. Its thick, powerful tail whipped the bobbing ranks of midget entities and through the wreckage of their vessels, scooping men and lumber from the Mississippi, tossing them for thirty yards or more to splashdown.

Few of them resurfaced, mostly staying underwater, swept away downstream.

How many left?

The creature men had named and named again from

bones turned into stone had no idea, could not even have framed the question in its mind. There were not many, clearly not enough to overpower it by force if there had been a hundred more on hand. The beast was in its native element and taking full advantage of it, while its puny challengers had no means to defend themselves against its wrath.

So why keep crushing, drowning, killing them?

Because an enemy, if it survived to fight another day, might find some way to win next time.

The beast tried to remember something that eluded it, some purpose it had fastened onto earlier, before the boats arrived to pepper it with insect stings. What had that been?

As if in answer to its silent thought, a tickling at its brain revived the buried memory. Cold talons dug into its brain, held on, and *squeezed.*

Remembering as if a veil of fog had lifted, the beast turned back toward the taunting beacon, leaving dazed survivors of its fierce attack to sink or swim.

Yancy Olson saw the right hook coming but had no time to react before it smashed into the left side of his face.

The whitecap leader toppled to his right, Hightower's left, with nothing but the river's gray-green water to prevent him ducking out of sight. He came up sputtering and fearless, outraged that the chief would try to beat him now, when both of them had vastly greater things to think about.

One vastly greater thing, that was.

"You dirty sumbitch!" Olson gargled, fighting back as best he could, the knuckles of his right fist glancing off

Hightower's forehead, sopping hair like seaweed hanging down.

It felt as if Yancy had punched a bonefish and accomplished nothing by it, other than bruising his hand. He had another swing in mind when Chief Hightower grabbed him by the throat with both hands, cutting off his air supply. Olson fought back, but feebly, slapping Hightower the way he'd seen girls tussle with each other, doing little or no damage.

Daylight still beat down upon the Mississippi, but the world was going black for Yancy Olson. Gouging at Hightower's strangling hands with his long fingernails and drawing blood, but still the chief kept up his fierce pressure on Yancy's windpipe. Slowly bringing down the final curtain.

Desperate, the whitecap leader started kicking underwater with his booted feet. The first try missed, but then the second, struck Highwater's thigh and put a startled grimace on the cop's face. Yancy tried again and hit a bull's eye, crushing the police chief's genitals with his left boot's toe. With a breathless squeal, Hightower lost his grip on Olson's throat and tried to thrash away from him, but Yancy wasn't giving up that easily.

He kicked the chief again, less strength behind it this time and off-target, then lurched forward, grabbing two handfuls of hair and shoving the chief's head below water. Using that grip, Yancy heaved forward, used his own torso to cover up the spot where Hightower was thrashing, squirming, desperate to breathe.

"Go on, then," Yancy taunted Hightower. "Suck in that water and for God's sake die!"

Just then, a shadow loomed above him and the man he meant to drown. Craning his neck, he saw the river monster poised above him, streaming water, already descending.

Suddenly, there was no time to scream.

"It's coming," Thorn alerted Finch. "Come around to ten o'clock."

"I'm working on it," Finch replied. "Feels like the rudder took a hit."

Thorn didn't want to think about that now, when he was looking at their probable last chance to end the fight that had already cost a score of lives by his count in the past few minutes. Time dragged, and he heard Finch cursing steadily, as *Sturgeon* responded sluggishly, in fits and starts.

In front of Gideon the furious *Basilosaurus* had apparently forgotten all about the occupants of three boats it had shattered and capsized. It wasn't hiding now, but speeding toward collision with the *Sturgeon* with its long sinuous back exposed above the river's surface, mouth agape.

That could be helpful for his one and only shot with the torpedo if it worked, if Finch could bring the *Sturgeon* into line with its rampaging enemy, if nothing else occurred to interrupt the creature's focus on the mental contact Thorn had reestablished.

Uncertainty was all he had to bank on, and that raised the odds that he would never see another sunset.

If that were the case, Thorn knew Obi Magoro would be fine, proprietor of the estate and its investments under the terms of Gideon's will, promoted from a trusted caretaker to Boston's richest African American.

As for the fate of Dinah Pilcher...well, if Thorn was crushed, drowned or devoured in the next few moments, he would never know.

"I make it thirty yards," he called to Finch.

"I almost got it," the freedman replied, voice straining as he fought the damaged rudder with one hand and kept the submarine's propellers turning with the other.

"You're close," Gideon granted, "but its closing fast."

More cursing and the sound of something scraping, grinding underneath the *Sturgeon*. If the rudder had been severed or smashed outright, Thorn surmised they couldn't turn at all. But if the shaft was bent from being dragged along the killer beast's full length, and if Thorn missed his last chance with the spar torpedo, Finch's work would all have been in vain.

"Closer!" Finch prodded his companion. "Twenty yards!"

"Doing the goddamn best I can!" Finch rasped.

"Fifteen!"

The *Sturgeon* gave a final jolt and then fell into line. Thorn saw the monster's maw yawning before him, hopefully lined up to meet the spar torpedo still invisible to him beneath the river's surface.

"Ten seconds! Hang onto something!"

"Like my lunch, you mean?" Incredibly, Finch laughed aloud.

"Coming!"

Thorn could not see the pronged torpedo slide into the prehistoric nightmare's mouth but felt the solid impact and a sense of moving backwards, driven by their enemy's great bulk and strong momentum. Up ahead, only the great mouth's lining and its fearful teeth now visible, Thorn had a sense of sharpened steel meeting soft flesh and tougher muscle, biting deep and taking hold.

"I think we've got it," he told Finch. "Can you reverse away from it?"

"I'll damn sure try!"

At first, Gideon thought they might be trapped, fangs that reminded him of saber blades gnashing against the *Sturgeon*'s prow. But then, painfully slow at first, accompanied by grating sounds of teeth scraping on rusty iron, the submarine began to back away, to free itself.

Almost.

The spar torpedo's harpoon head still linked them to the monster, holding them in place.

Gideon pulled a lever then *Sturgeon* seemed to find new energy, powering in reverse while its assailant thrashed and shook its head, trying to lose the pain inside its mouth.

If gnashing teeth shredded the cable linking Thorn to the torpedo's aged detonator, it would all have been in vain.

"What's safe, as far as distance?" he asked Finch.

The cable's thirty-odd feet long," Finch answered back. "Beyond that, your guess is as good as mine."

Unable to wait any longer, Thorn reached for a second cable that would trigger the explosive. If he had misjudged the distance, they might be obliterated by the coming blast —or else, the line might have been severed, meaning they had sacrificed their lives for naught.

"Firing!" he snapped. Thinking at the same time, *I hope!*

The detonation, when it happened, sounded like a sledgehammer striking the *Sturgeon*'s bow. The whole submersible shuddered, as if with ague, and everything before him turned to crimson, blotting out Thorn's view of their attacker, of the Mississippi, and the boats already ravaged in the monster's wake.

There came another panicked moment when the beast appeared to rise above them, maybe trying to destroy them with its plunging bulk, but as the scope's lens cleared Thorn saw that it was nearly headless, nothing but a ragged remnant of its lower jaw still barely fastened to its neck.

"Bullseye!" said Thorn.

Behind him, Finch was praising Jesus and a list of saints too numerous for Gideon to memorize.

That babbling went on for another moment before Thorn broke into it, asking, "What are the odds of getting back to shore?"

"No problem," Finch replied, laughing again. "After all that, I reckon I could sail this baby all the way to Africa."

Thorn smiled at that and said, "Right now, I'll settle for dry land."

EPILOGUE

NATCHEZ: JUNE 24, 1877

"You're pulling out today, then? Jubal Kenfield asked.

"Right after breakfast," Thorn confirmed.

He had already spent some early time with Belle and Shadow, mentally preparing them for crossing to Vidalia on whichever ferry still survived and was available for hire.

"The meal's on me," Kenfield announced. "I wish we could have had more time together."

"Maybe another time," said Gideon. "I want to go before a new chief of police turns up."

"From what I hear," the newsman said, "that might require some time."

"No volunteers?"

"Oh, plenty, I imagine. But it seems our governor has had a change of heart about the local party structure. More specifically, Grover Arquette."

"Dissatisfied with money spent?"

"It's worse than that. There's talk about a 'full investigation' if you can believe it."

"Call me skeptical," Thorn said. "Some things were made to be swept under any rug that's handy."

"Well, at least I'll get the truth out in another 'Extra' for the *Independent*."

"If they let you," Thorn replied.

"Just let them try and stop me."

"Careful what you wish for," Gideon advised. "Somebody told me recently that Mississippi's barely part of the United States."

"That needs to change," said Kenfield. "Maybe not in my lifetime, but I can make a start."

"Good luck with that."

"You've likely helped, as well."

"All I did was go fishing," Gideon replied.

That brought a full-blown laugh from Kenfield, making early morning shoppers pause and turn to state at him on Silver Street.

"Do you suppose that book about your life will ever go to print?" the publisher inquired.

"Anything's possible," Thorn said, and felt his thoughts drawn back to Dinah Pilcher in Boston.

"Do you really believe that?" Kenfield asked.

"Well," Gideon amended, "*almost* anything."

A LOOK AT WARPATH BY MICHAEL NEWTON

In the sun-scorched wilds of Arizona Territory, 1877, settlers are dying brutal, inexplicable deaths: livestock slaughtered, ranches razed, and whispers of a diablero—an ancient demon summoned to sow chaos—ripple through the region. When Yaqui shamans raise the creature to drive white colonists from tribal lands, a powder keg of fear and prejudice ignites.

Enter Gideon Thorn, still recovering from the wounds of his last confrontation with the unknown. As Thorn follows the trail of carnage across the desert, it becomes clear this is more than superstition...and the creature he hunts may be unlike any he's faced before.

But to stop the slaughter, Thorn must not only confront the supernatural but also navigate the volatile tensions between settlers and Native peoples—before the violence explodes into full-blown war.

Warpath is a haunting blend of western myth, indigenous legend, and supernatural terror...where survival means standing firm against evil, even when it wears many faces.

THANK YOU

Thank you for taking the time to read *Rip Tide*. If you enjoyed it, please consider telling your friends or posting a short review. Word of mouth is an author's best friend and much appreciated.

Thank you.
Michael Newton

ABOUT THE AUTHOR

A California native, Michael Newton published over 215 books under his own name and various pseudonyms since 1977. He began writing professionally as a "ghost" for author Don Pendleton on the best-selling Executioner series. With 104 episodes published to date, Newton nearly tripled the number of Mack Bolan novels completed by creator Pendleton himself.

www.ingramcontent.com/pod-product-compliance
Lightning Source LLC
LaVergne TN
LVHW040218110826
845146LV00005B/1340

9798895676110